LOVE'S RETALIATION

LOVE'S MAGIC SERIES BOOK 10

BETTY MCLAIN

Copyright (C) 2019 Betty McLain

Layout design and Copyright (C) 2019 by Creativia

Published 2019 by Creativia (www.creativia.org)

Edited by Marilyn Wagner

Cover art by Cover Mint

This book is dedicated to the ones who are brave enough to pursue their own true love.

CHAPTER 1

$\mathcal{T}$imothy Sorason was sitting by his friend, and roommate's, hospital bed. His friend, Willard Murdoc, was sleeping. The hospital staff had been keeping him sedated since he had been brought to the hospital by ambulance. They were trying to keep him calm. Will's face was blistered and red. The doctors had covered his eyes with gauze to protect them until they could see how much damage had been done.

Called by the police, Will's parents rushed into the room and hurried over to Will's bedside. Tim moved out of the way, so they could get closer.

Cam Murdoc, Will's father, turned to Tim. "What happened? The police said he was trying to take the magic mirror. Why would he do something like that?"

"He wasn't planning on keeping it. He just wanted to keep it away from Alison. She told him she was going to the museum to look in the mirror. She wanted to see if Will was really her true love. Will panicked. He is crazy about Alison and the thought of her seeing anyone else in the mirror made him lose all reason. He thought if he could just keep Alison from looking in it for a while, she would forget about it," Tim tried to explain.

"How did he get hurt?" asked Lucy Murdoc.

"He had the mirror and was on his way out. I was waiting outside for him. He must have triggered a silent alarm. When he heard the sirens, he panicked and dropped the mirror. It broke in to two pieces. A bright light came out of both pieces and struck Will in the face. It looked like lightning," said Tim with a shudder.

"You said the mirror broke?" asked Cam.

"Yes, I saw it break. The police didn't believe me, because, when they found the mirror, after Will was in the ambulance, it was in one piece again, I don't know how to explain it, but I saw the mirror break and send two streams of light to Will," said Tim shaking his head.

"Are the police going to file any charges?" asked Cam.

"I don't know. They had me down at the police station for questioning, but they didn't keep me long. I think it will be up to the museum to press charges," said Tim.

"Does Alison know that Will is in the hospital?" asked Lucy.

"I don't know. I have not called her," said Tim with a frown. "If she had not been teasing Will, he would not have tried to take the mirror, and he would not have gotten hurt. I know he thinks he is in love with her, but I think he needs to slow down and get to know her better."

"I think you are a good friend," said Lucy, patting his arm. "Thank you for caring."

Dr. Marcus Drake entered the room. The Murdocs moved away from the bed so he could check on Will.

"How is he, Doc?" asked Cam.

"It will be morning before we can check his eyes," said Dr. Drake. "We have called an eye specialist to be here when we take his bandages off to check them."

Marcus turned to face the Murdocs. He held out his hand to first one and then the other. "I'm Dr. Marcus Drake. I have been looking after your son since he was brought in. I think the damage is only on his face. It looks like a flash burn, similar to a lightning strike. Tim told me about the mirror. I can't say one way or the other about the mirror. It may have been reflecting off something. We have no way of knowing, so we will just have to leave it up to the police to investigate it. Will is not going to wake up tonight. He was given a sedative. Why don't you all go home and come back in the morning?" Dr. Drake turned and left.

"I'm not leaving my son here by himself," declared Lucy.

Cam put his arm around her shoulder. "Why don't you go on home and call David and Mike? I'll stay here with Will. You can go home, too, Tim. I will let you know if there is any change."

"I could stay a while longer if you need to drive Mrs. Murdoc home," said Tim.

"Thank you, Tim. I'll drive Lucy home and be right back," said Cam.

"Take your time," said Tim. "I'm in no hurry."

The Murdocs left after Lucy gave Tim a hug. Tim settled down at Will's bedside to wait.

Shortly after the Murdocs left, the door eased open and Alison Street entered. "Alison, what are you doing here?" asked Tim, startled.

Alison walked over to Will's bedside and stood, gazing at his face covered in bandages.

"I heard about Will on the news. I came to see how he is doing," said Alison.

"You just missed his parents," remarked Tim.

"Yes, I know. I waited for them to leave," said Alison.

"Why?" asked Tim, looking at her hard.

"I was afraid they would blame me for Will being hurt," said Alison. "Did he really try to take the magic mirror?"

"After you told him you were going to see if you could see your true love in the mirror, what did you expect him to do?" asked Tim.

"I was only teasing him," said Alison. "I never thought he would take me seriously."

"Well, he did," said Tim. "Why don't you go ahead and look in the mirror. If you are going to look for true love in the mirror, you must not have the same feelings for Will as he has for you. Why do you have to keep stringing him along and getting his hopes up?"

"I care about Will," protested Alison.

Tim shook his head. "You only like the idea of having a boyfriend who is crazy about you, to flaunt in front of all of your friends."

Alison sighed and ignored Tim's words. She looked at Tim and then looked down at Will again. "Are you going to tell me how he is?" asked Alison.

"They won't know how bad it is until they remove his bandages in the morning," said Tim. "They can't tell how badly his eyes were damaged until then."

"Are you going to stay all night?' asked Alison.

"No, I'm staying until Mr. Murdoc gets back. He went to take Mrs. Murdoc home," remarked Tim.

"I guess I had better go," said Alison nervously. "Will you let me know how Will is doing in the morning?"

Tim shrugged his shoulder. "I'll let you know when I can."

"Thank you," said Alison, as she left.

Tim turned back to Will with a sigh. "Buddy, I hope you get over the obsession you have with Alison. She is in no way ready to settle into a committed relationship."

Alison had mentioned seeing about Will on the news. Tim took the TV remote and clicked the power button. He turned the sound down low so it wouldn't disturb Will and flipped through the channels until he found one telling news. The news crew was out in front of the museum. They were trying to get a statement from the lady in charge.

"I told you, I do not have any details about the attempted break in. If you want anything further, talk to the police," she said. The lady turned and went back into the museum and closed the door.

"There you have it, folks. Mrs. Valerie Drake, the museum curator, has denied any knowledge of the attempted break in. This is SECC news, signing off." The news person cut off and the broadcast was transferred back to the station. Tim turned the TV off.

The door opened and Tim turned and watched Mr. Murdoc enter the room. He came over to the bed, and Tim got up so he could have the chair at his son's bedside.

"I'll see you first thing in the morning," said Tim.

"Good night, Tim, and thank you," said Mr. Murdoc.

"There are no thanks needed. He is my friend," said Tim as he turned and left.

Mr. Murdoc looked at his son with a sigh and bowed his head to say a prayer. He raised his head and looked at Will. He was so young, too young to tie himself to a relationship with such an immature girl. He hoped this accident would give Will a chance to understand this.

While Mr. Murdoc was sitting at his son's bedside, Tim was entering the room he and Will shared at the college. It was a very lonely place without Will there. He shook his head. He had tried to talk Will out of his hair-brained idea. Maybe he had not tried hard enough to stop him. It was going to be a long time until morning. He lay down on his bed. Maybe he could rest a while. There was no way he was going to be able to sleep. The next thing he knew, the alarm went off. He turned it off and looked at the clock. It was six o' clock. Tim quickly jumped in the shower and, putting on clean clothes, headed for the hospital. He went through a drive-through on the way and picked up two coffees. He handed one to Mr. Murdoc when he entered Will's room.

"Thank you, Tim," said Mr. Murdoc.

The door of Will's room opened and David and Mike, Will's two brothers, entered. "How's he doing?" asked Mike.

"He's still asleep," remarked Mr. Murdoc.

"Hi, Tim," said David.

"Hi," said Tim.

"How did Will come up with such a hair-brained scheme?" asked Mike. "How did he get into the museum?"

"He had been sitting around, brooding about Alison, saying she was going to look in the mirror. She said she wanted to see if Will was her true love. The more he thought about the mirror, the worse his mood became. He just snapped. I tried to talk him out of it, but he was determined to keep the mirror away from Alison. He said if he could keep her from looking in the mirror for a while, she would forget all about it," said Tim. "He had a skeleton key. When he tried it, it opened the door to the museum. All he had to do was walk right in."

David shook his head. "Didn't he realize it would be better to find out how Alison really felt before they became any more involved?"

"Like I said, he wasn't thinking. He was just reacting," remarked Tim. "I think when his key opened the door; he took it as a sign he was supposed to go on in."

Will stirred and moaned. Everyone stopped and looked at him. When he raised his hand to his face, His dad caught his hand and held it.

"You have bandages over your eyes, Will. The doctor will take them off in a little while," said Cam.

"Dad," whispered Will. "What happened? Where am I?"

"You are in the hospital. You had an accident. Just relax and wait for the doctor. He can tell you more," said Cam Murdoc.

"Yeah, little brother, take it easy," said David.

"David, what are you doing here?" asked Will.

"Where else do you think I would be when my little brother is in the hospital?" asked David.

"Yeah," agreed Mike. "We have to make sure you don't get spoiled with all these pretty nurses making a fuss over you."

"Mike, you are here, too?" said Will. "Is Mom here?"

"She will be back soon. The doctor sent her home last night," said Cam.

"Is Tim here?" asked Will.

"I'm right here," said Tim.

"Have you heard from Alison?" asked Will.

Tim's lips tightened. "She came by last night for a few minutes." Cam gave Tim an inquiring look. "She came by while you were taking Mrs. Murdoc home."

"Is she alright?" asked Will.

"She is fine. Don't worry about her. Relax and wait for the doctor to tell you how you are. When you get out of here, there will be time enough to deal with Alison," said Tim.

Will settled back with a sigh. "I guess you're right," he said.

Lucy Murdoc entered the hospital room and hurried to Will's bedside. "Will, you're awake! How are you feeling?" she asked, taking his hand.

"Mom, I don't feel much of anything except some itching on my face. I'm glad you're here," said Will.

"Where else would I be?" asked Lucy. "My baby gets hurt; of course, I'm going to be here."

"Mom, I'm not a baby," protested Will when both David and Mike laughed.

"You'll always be my baby," said Lucy giving both David and Mike a glare. They both quickly straightened their faces and tried to look innocent.

Lucy spotted Tim and smiled at him. "Good morning. Tim."

"Good morning, Mrs. Murdoc," said Tim.

"I'm glad Will has a friend like you to be here for him," said Lucy Murdoc

"Will would do the same for me," replied Tim.

"Of course, he would," agreed Lucy Murdoc with a smile.

CHAPTER 2

*T*he hospital door opened, and Dr. Drake entered followed by another doctor. He nodded hello to everyone. "Mr. and Mrs. Murdoc, this is Dr. Judy Loren. She is an eye specialist. She is going to check on Will's eyes when we remove the bandages."

Dr. Loren came to Will's bedside and shook hands with Lucy and Cam. She nodded to the three men present.

"These are Will's brothers, David and Mike, and his best friend, Tim," said Lucy when she noticed Dr. Loren looking at the men. Dr. Loren nodded and smiled at the guys. They all smiled back at her with a nod. A nurse came in with an instrument tray and the guys moved over to the window, out of the way.

"Could one of you close the window shade?" asked Dr. Loren. "The light may be too bright when we take off the bandages." David turned and closed it. . Cam and Lucy moved back out of the way, but stayed close to the end of the bed, so they could see what was happening.

The nurse raised the head of the bed so the doctor could better reach Will's head and handed Dr. Drake the scissors. He carefully cut the bandages around Will's eyes and started unwrapping them from around his head. Dr. Loren held the pads in place under the gauze. When the gauze was out of the way, she, carefully, removed the pads.

Will blinked and stared toward the end of the bed where his parents were standing.

"What can you see, Will?" asked Dr. Loren.

"It's very blurry, but I can just make out my parents," said Will.

"Good," said Dr. Loren. She started studying Will's eyes with her instruments. "Will, you have a very bad flash burn. Your eyesight will get better, but we won't know how much for a few days. I'm not going to wrap them up again, but I am going to give you these dark glasses. I want you to wear the glasses at all times except when you are sleeping. It's very important to keep bright light from your eyes. I am also going to have the nurse administer some eye drops to keep your eyes lubricated. I will check on you tomorrow. We need you to stay in the hospital for a couple of days."

"Okay, Doctor, thanks," said Will. Dr. Loren turned and nodded to everyone as she left.

Dr. Drake moved up to the place vacated by Dr. Loren. He and the nurse applied cold compresses on Will's face to help with the burn. "These compresses need to be removed in thirty minutes. You can wait an hour and apply them again for thirty more minutes," Dr. Drake instructed the nurse.

"Yes, Dr. Drake," said the nurse.

Dr. Drake reassured the Murdocs and left. The nurse left to get more cold compresses for Will's face. David and Mike came over and each gave Will an awkward hug.

"I'll see you later. I have to get to work. You do what the doctor says, so you can get out of here," said Mike.

"Yeah, no getting up and chasing after these pretty nurses," said David as the nurse returned and grinned at him. "I'll see you after work."

After Mike and David left, Tim came forward. "Don't you have class?" asked Will.

"I just have one class today. I can get the notes from Penny," said Tim.

Will turned to his dad. "You don't have to stay, Dad. I'll be fine. There is nothing you can do, but sit here," said Will.

Cam looked thoughtful for a minute, then, shrugged his shoulders.

"Maybe you are right. I know it can be irritating to have someone sit and stare at you."

Cam turned and hugged Lucy. "You call me if there is any problem," he said.

"I will," promised Lucy.

After Cam left, Will looked to where Lucy was sitting. "You can stop right there, Will Murdoc. I'm not going anywhere. You are just going to have to put up with me," she declared.

Tim laughed and Will joined in. "I wasn't trying to get rid of you Mom. I hate being such a bother to everyone. I don't know what I was thinking to pull such a stupid stunt."

"We all pull stupid stunts in our lives, Will. The trick is to realize how stupid it was and correct your mistake," said Lucy.

"How do I correct the mistake? I can't turn back time," said Will.

"No, you can't, but you can apologize to everyone involved, including the magic mirror, and offer to make up for what you did," said Lucy.

"You want me to apologize to the magic mirror?" exclaimed Will.

"Why not?" asked Lucy. "You were trying to interfere with it doing its job. Don't you think it deserves an apology?"

"I suppose so, but I doubt the museum will let me anywhere near the magic mirror," said Will.

"You never know unless you ask," said Lucy with a faint smile. "One of life's most valuable lessons is learning to face your mistakes and to make things better by making up for them."

Dr. Marcus Drake was keeping his wife Valerie updated on Will Murdoc's condition. He told her what he had overheard about why Will had broken into the museum and tried to take the magic mirror.

"There has been a lot of attention shown to the magic mirror since the news articles were published," said Valerie.

"It has stirred people's imagination," agreed Marcus. "Most of them don't really believe in the mirror, but they can't resist checking it out."

"It seems a shame for Will to have his life damaged because of his bad judgment," said Valerie.

"What can you do about it?" asked Marcus.

"I don't know. The police have been after me to press charges. I told them I would think about it. I need to talk to Will. I can't make a decision until I understand him better. I need to know if this is a one-time thing or if he makes a habit of pulling stunts such as these," Valerie said, thoughtfully.

"He seems like a good kid to me," said Marcus. "I think he deserves a second chance."

"How long will he be in the hospital?" asked Valerie.

"At least a couple more days," said Marcus. "Dr. Loren wants to check on his eyes a couple more times before he leaves the hospital."

"Maybe I'll pay him a visit," said Valerie.

"Let me know when you want to visit, and I'll take you by and introduce you," said Marcus.

"Alright, let me know when you think he is ready for visitors," said Valerie.

Marcus pulled Valerie into his lap as she passed him. "I'll keep it in mind. Right now, I have other things on my mind," said Marcus, pulling her close for a kiss.

"My favorite way to pass the time," agreed Valerie, returning his kiss with a smile.

The next morning, when Dr. Drake made his rounds, he examined Will's eyes and face. After checking him over, Dr. Drake told Will and Mrs. Murdoc there was a little less redness on Will's face, but he still had a lot of healing to do.

"How would you feel about a visitor from the museum stopping by to see you, Will?" asked Dr. Drake.

Will shrugged his shoulder. "Sure, I need to tell them how sorry I am for breaking into the museum," said Will. "My mom tells me I need to apologize to the magic mirror, also." Dr. Drake looked thoughtful. "What do you think, Doc?' asked Will.

"It couldn't hurt. It might help. You have to mean it though. It would make matters worse if you are not sincere," replied Dr. Drake.

Will tried hard to study Dr. Drake's face. "You really believe it is a magic mirror," said Will.

"Yes, I do. There are all kinds of magic in the world. A lot of people let the magic pass them by. Others barely touch on the magic. If you believe in the magic, it will make your life much better. Each person must decide their own beliefs. A person with magic in their life, is in for a wonderful ride. Have a good morning, Will." Dr. Drake and his nurse continued with morning rounds.

Will thought about Dr. Drake's words while he rested his eyes. His words made a lot of sense.

Dr. Loren came by to check on Will's eyes. She did not have much to say. According to Dr. Loren, there had been no change in his condition. Will only saw images as blurs, the shapes were there, but they were hard to make out. When Dr. Drake made his evening rounds, he brought his wife, Valerie with him to be introduced to Will.

"Hi, Will, I have a visitor for you," said Dr. Drake. "This is my wife, Valerie; she is Curator at the museum."

"Hello, Mrs. Drake, I'm glad you are here," said Will. "I wanted to tell you how sorry I am for trying to take the magic mirror. It was a very stupid idea. I should have trusted in my feelings. If Alison and I were not meant to be together, I had no right to try to force the outcome to suit myself. I know saying I'm sorry can't make up for breaking into the museum. My mom has already told me I need to apologize to everyone involved, including the magic mirror."

Valerie smiled. "Your mom is a very smart lady," said Valerie. "When you are well enough to go home, have whoever is taking you home bring you by the museum. I will let you speak to the magic mirror. If the mirror forgives you, the museum will not press charges. We will figure another way for you to work off your debt."

"How will you know if the magic mirror accepts my apology?" asked Will looking very confused.

Valerie laughed. "My parents brought this magic mirror and two others over from Italy. There have been many miracles performed by the mirrors. If the magic mirror accepts your apology, you will know. It will find a way to let you know. There is just one thing, Will, make sure you are sincere when you talk to the mirror. If you are not sincere, it will only make matters worse."

"I promise to be very sincere," said Will. "Thank you for coming by to see me. I promise I will never do such a stupid thing again."

"I am very glad for a chance to speak to you. Rest and get better. I will look forward to seeing you soon," said Valerie.

Valerie and Dr. Drake turned and left Will's hospital room. They stopped in the hall to speak with his mom. She was on her way back to his room from the cafeteria. After briefly speaking to Valerie and Marcus, she returned to Will's hospital room.

"It was very nice of Mrs. Drake to come by and see you," she said to Will. "She seems like a real nice lady."

"Yes, it was. She told me to come by the museum when I get released and she will let me talk to the magic mirror," said Will.

His mom looked up startled. "You asked her about talking to the mirror?"

"Yes, she told me I could apologize to the magic mirror. If it accepts my apology, they won't press charges against me for breaking into the museum. She really believes in the magic mirror," said Will.

Lucy Murdoc smiled. "There is a lot of magic in the world, Will. You have to believe and accept it."

"Yes, Ma'am," said Will as he lay back and closed his eyes to rest.

CHAPTER 3

*W*ill's brothers, David and Mike, came by to see him after work.
"Dad said to tell you he would be by later. He wanted to go home and get cleaned up first," said David.

"How are your eyes? Are you seeing any clearer?" asked Mike.

"Everything is still blurry," said Will. "The doctor said it would take a few days before they could see how much damage has been done."

While they were talking, Alison peered around the door into the room. Will heard the door open and looked toward it. Mike and David both turned and looked to see who had entered. When they saw Alison, they smiled and said hello.

"Hi," said Alison. "I came by to see how Will is doing."

"I'm okay," said Will. "Alison, these are my brothers, David and Mike. Guys, this is a friend of mine, Alison Street."

"It's nice to meet you, Alison," said Mike. He went over to greet Alison and, taking her hand, led her to Will's bedside.

Alison glanced around nervously. Alison glanced at Will, then looked away quickly when she saw the redness and blisters on his face.

"Thank you for stopping by. Tim told me you stopped by when I was first brought in," said Will.

"I heard about it on the news. I had to see if it was true. I could hardly believe what I was hearing," said Alison.

"Yes, it's true," said Will. "I pulled a stupid stunt."

"We all do stupid things when we are your age," said David. "It's a rite of passage, part of growing up. You wouldn't be normal if you didn't do something stupid at least once."

Will smiled at David. "I bet you guys will be teasing me about it for years to come."

"Sure we will," agreed Mike. "It's in the big brother creed. We wouldn't be doing our job if we didn't remind you of all the things you want to forget,"

Alison smiled at their banter. They reminded her of her and her sisters. They always teased each other the same way. She was sure if anything happened to her; both of her sisters would be right there beside her, cheering her up.

"I need to go," said Alison. "I'll try to get in to see you tomorrow. Take care of yourself."

"I will. Thank you for coming by," said Will.

Alison squeezed his hand and waved to David and Mike as she turned and left the room.

Mike looked at Will and saw him frowning. "What's wrong, Will? I thought you were into Alison," said Mike.

"I thought I was, too. Since all of this happened, I have had time to think about Alison. I think I was letting an infatuation rule me. I don't know how I feel now. I think I need to wait and see how things go with my eyes before I consider how my relationship with Alison is going," Will sighed, deeply.

"You are young. There is no need to rush into anything. Take your time and be sure," said David. "If she is meant for you, she will wait for you to be sure and to be sure, herself."

"You boys can head on over to the house," said Cam entering the room. "Your mom said to tell you supper is waiting."

"Yes, sir," agreed Mike and David as they told Will good night and left.

"How are you doing?" asked Cam going to Will's bedside.

"The doctor said there had been no change, but I can see a little clearer," said Will.

"Good, you know how you are feeling better than anyone. Your mom said she would be here after she feeds your brothers."

Will smiled. "She doesn't need to stay with me all night. I will be fine. All I'm going to do is sleep. I don't need anyone to sit and watch me sleep. If there is any change, you guys are just a phone call away."

"I'll talk to your mom, but you know how stubborn she is when she makes up her mind," said Cam.

"Yeah, I know, maybe I can talk her into going home," said Will.

"Maybe," agreed Cam. "Has Tim been here?"

"Yes, he left earlier, before Mike and David arrived. I think I convinced him to get some rest and go to class tomorrow. I told him he would have to take notes for both of us," Will smiled.

"Good, we wouldn't want you to fall behind in your classes," agreed Cam.

"Tim has already talked to the teachers. They agreed to give him our assignments and let us do makeup work. We will be fine," said Will.

"Tim is a good friend and he has a good head on his shoulders. He is going to be fine in whatever field he decides to pursue. You lucked up getting him for a roommate and friend," said Cam.

"Yes, I did," agreed Will.

The nurse came in with another cold compress for Will's face. Cam moved away from the bed to give her room to work. "Is his face any better?" asked Cam.

"The compresses are mostly to keep his swelling down and to help with pain and itching. It's going to take time for his face to heal," said the nurse. "If you are going to be here a while, would you remove the compresses from his face in thirty minutes? We are very busy on the floor right now," she said to Cam.

"Sure, I'll take care of them," said Cam. The nurse smiled a thank you and hurried away. Cam settled back at Will's bedside to wait for the time to pass. "Has Alison been by today?" asked Cam.

"Yes, sir, she came by while Mike and David were here," replied Will. "She didn't stay long."

"Some people are nervous around hospitals," remarked Cam.

"Maybe," agreed Will. "Dad, I'm sorry for causing so much trouble. I don't know what came over me. It was like I had something inside of me, driving me on." Will shuddered.

Cam took his hand and squeezed it. "We all do things in the heat of the moment. The main thing is to learn from our mistakes and try to do the best we can to correct them. Before you act on your feelings, you need to stop, take a breath, and think about what you are doing," said Cam.

"I know, and I promise I will never, ever try breaking into a building again. If I lose my keys, I'll call a locksmith," Will declared.

Cam laughed. "If you lose your keys, you can call me. I probably have copies of all your keys. What I don't have, your mom will have."

Will smiled. "I'll have to remember that," he said.

"Is your car parked at the dorm?" asked Cam.

"Yes, Tim drove it to the dorm and parked it for me," said Will.

"Good," said Cam.

After the thirty minutes were up, Cam took the compresses off of Will's face and dropped them into the basin the nurse left. He sat back down and watched as Will's eyes closed sleepily. While Will slept, Cam thought about all of the happenings of the last few days. Never had he thought one of his sons would ever try to break into a building. It was hard to imagine Will even thinking about such a thing. He and Lucy had tried to raise the boys to respect the law and to have respect for other people's property. Even though Will had not been planning to keep the magic mirror, to break in and take it went against everything he had been taught.

Lucy entered quietly. She saw Will sleeping and, leaning over, kissed Cam. "How is he doing?" she asked quietly.

"He is about the same," said Cam. "He insists we need to go home instead of staying here all night. He said he will be sleeping, and we are a phone call away if we are needed."

Lucy sighed. "Maybe he is right. I hate leaving him here alone, but they will probably give him something to make him sleep. We can come back early in the morning."

Cam squeezed her hand. "Another day and he will be able to go home. You can fuss over him then."

"Mom," said Will stirring.

"I'm right here, Will," said Lucy. She reached over and took his hand in her hand.

"How are you?" asked Lucy.

"I'm fine. Why don't you and Dad head on home. I am very sleepy. I will probably not wake up until the nurse wakes me for medicine," said Will.

"Okay, Will, we will head home, but if you need us for anything, you have the nurse call us," said Lucy.

"I will." promised Will.

Lucy leaned over and kissed his cheek and Cam rubbed his shoulder, then they left and headed for home, while Will closed his eyes and went back to sleep.

They parted outside the hospital, each going to their own car to drive home.

Alison, sitting in her car watching, saw them leave. She exited her car and took the elevator to the floor where Will's room was located. She looked around, and seeing no one around, headed for Will's room.

Will stirred and looked toward the door when he heard it open. He looked hard at the shadowy figure. "Alison, is that you?" he asked.

"Yes, it's me. I waited until everyone left. I wanted to talk to you alone," she said. She walked over to Will's bedside and took his hand.

"What do you want to talk about?" asked Will giving her hand a squeeze.

"I wanted to tell you how sorry I am for teasing you about the magic mirror. I never had any intention of going to look in the mirror. I did not believe in a mirror being able to show people their true love. I was just putting on a show for my friends, I had no idea you would take me seriously. I am sorry you got hurt because of me," said Alison.

"I did not get hurt because of you. This is not your fault. It is my fault for making such bad choices. I should have had more confidence in myself and you. I did something I should not have done, and I am paying the price. I care about you, and I know we are friends. Whether we will ever be more than friends remains to be seen. I realize I cannot force feelings from you or myself," said Will.

"I just wanted you to know how sorry I am. I hope everything is going to be alright," said Alison.

"I will be fine in a few days," assured Will. "Don't worry. You need to get back to your dorm. It is getting late. Thanks for coming by."

"Okay," Alison leaned over and kissed his cheek and then left.

Will sighed and closed his eyes. His mind was so active; it was hard to get back to sleep.

"Still awake?" asked the nurse cheerfully as she entered his room.

"Yes," answered Will.

The nurse took two sleeping pills from a container and handed Will a glass of water to help swallowing them. Will pulled the blanket up and closed his eyes as the nurse left. He was soon asleep.

Alison arrived back at her dorm room. Her roommate was studying. When she entered, her roommate looked up at her.

"How's Will?" asked Beth.

"He is doing okay, I guess. It's hard to tell with all the red blisters on his face and the dark glasses he is wearing. Of course, he always says he is fine. He doesn't want anyone worrying about him," replied Alison.

Beth frowned. "I told you he wasn't going to like you teasing him about the magic mirror."

"I know. I should have listened. Things seem different between us now. I think Will's feelings for me have changed," said Alison.

"Maybe he is just in shock from being hurt," said Beth.

"Maybe," agreed Alison. "I don't know. I know Tim doesn't like me. He told me to go and look in the magic mirror. He said it was my fault that Will got hurt. He is right, if I had not been teasing Will about the mirror, he never would have tried to take it."

"Maybe you should look in the magic mirror. If there is any chance there is someone else out there for you, it is better to know now," said Beth.

"I don't know," said Alison. "I have feelings for Will. I just don't know if they are the forever kind of feelings."

"Well, for both of your sakes, there should be no doubts. The museum will be closed for a few days. When it opens back up, you and I are going to pay the magic mirror a visit," declared Beth. "I would like to know if there is someone out there for me."

Alison agreed, and she and Beth settled down to do their studying. They both had a lot on their minds, and they had to concentrate very hard to understand what they were trying to learn.

Beth looked at Alison thoughtfully. She had always wondered about Alison's feelings for Will, but she had tried not to interfere. She did not know if what she was feeling was real or just wishful thinking. She had met Will at the same time as Alison, but he had hardly noticed her. He had only had eyes for Alison. She had dazzled him.

Beth had not let anyone see her feelings for Will. They were her closely guarded secret. She wanted Will to be happy. If there was any chance Alison and Will were meant to be together, her feelings would never be acknowledged, but if Alison was meant for someone else, maybe she had a chance with Will. She would have to wait and see.

CHAPTER 4

Two days later, Will was being dismissed from the hospital. Cam and Lucy were waiting for him at the front door when the nurse brought him down in a wheelchair. He was wearing the dark glasses Dr. Loren had given to him. He still had very blurry vision, but with a great deal of effort, he was able to see slightly.

Cam helped Will into the back seat and helped him fasten his seat belt. Lucy was in the passenger side in the front seat. Cam went around the car, after helping Will, and entered the driver's seat.

"Could you stop by the museum on the way home?" asked Will.

"Are you sure you want to go by the museum now?' asked Cam. "Shouldn't you wait a day or so?"

"No, I told Mrs. Drake I would come by as soon as I was released from the hospital. I'm sure Dr. Drake has told her I would be released today. I don't want her to think I'm not serious about being sorry for breaking into the museum," explained Will.

"Okay, the museum it is," agreed Cam. He drove straight to the museum and parked right in front of the door. He went around the car to help Will out and into the museum.

"Hello, Will," said Valerie coming forward to greet him. She also turned and greeted Cam and Lucy. "If you will come with me, I have put a chair in front of the mirror so you can sit and talk to it."

"Thank you, Mrs. Drake," said Will.

They all followed Valerie into the next room, where the magic mirror was on display. Cam helped Will to the seat in front of the mirror, and he, Lucy, and Valerie moved away to let him talk to the mirror.

Will took off his dark glasses and looked at the mirror. He hardly knew what to say. He felt a little funny sitting here, getting ready to talk to a mirror. He shrugged. It had to be done. "I'm Will. I'm the one who broke in here and tried to take you. I'm very sorry. I realize I had no right trying to stop my girlfriend from pursuing her destiny. I have no right to force my vision of the future onto anyone else. Love must be freely given. It cannot be forced. I can't change my bad decision. I can only say I will do better in the future and I am very sorry for trying to stop you from doing your job."

Will sat still looking at the mirror. His parents stood over to the side with Valerie Drake and waited to see what was going to happen next. All of a sudden, a soft light shot out from the mirror and covered Will. Everyone gasped. Will sat there, with his eyes closed, enjoying the feel of love washing over him. When the light cleared, Will turned and smiled at his parents and Valerie.

"I guess the mirror forgave me," said Will.

Cam and Lucy gasped, and Valerie smiled. The redness on Will's face was completely gone and his eyes were clear in his smiling face. "I would say the mirror has forgiven you," agreed Valerie. "Now all we have to do is decide how you are going to make up for breaking into the museum. I should tell you we have had the lock changed on the door. I wanted to be sure the skeleton key could no longer open it. If one skeleton key worked on it, others might as well."

Will stopped smiling. "I am sorry about using the key to get in. I will do whatever you think is fair to make up for it," said Will.

Valerie was thoughtful for a minute as she turned the problem over in her mind. "Do you have classes on the weekends?" she asked.

"No, Ma'am, my weekends are free," said Will.

"How about you work here, in the museum, on Saturday and Sunday after church, for the next three months? We are closed on Sunday, but you can put out new stock," said Valerie.

Will stood up and went over and held out his hand to Valerie. "I will be here Saturday," he said.

Valerie shook his hand with a smile. We open at nine. One of your jobs will be to keep an eye on the magic mirror and keep it safe."

"I will keep it very safe," agreed Will. "I think we need all of the magic we can get in our lives, but the magic is for everyone, not just a few."

"Here, Here," agreed Lucy, giving Will a hug. "Thank you, Mrs. Drake for not turning Will over to the police."

"You're welcome, If the magic mirror can give Will another chance, who am I to argue?" agreed Valerie.

They all said goodbye, and the Murdocs left. Since Will was completely healed, they did not need to go straight home, so they decided to go out for a celebratory lunch. Will kept looking around at everything.

"Everything is so bright," he said. "You never know how great everything looks until you see it through a blur."

"Should we go by the hospital and let Dr. Drake know you have your eyesight back?" asked Lucy.

"I'll go by tomorrow, after class," said Will. "I'm sure Mrs. Drake will tell him what happened."

"I guess you are right," agreed Lucy.

"No," said Cam. "We will go by after lunch. You cannot start putting things off, Will."

"You are right, Dad. I have to show Mrs. Drake I mean what I say. I am going to do better and I will stop and think before I act," said Will. "If either of you see me sliding back into my old ways, just remind me of this."

Will sent Tim a text letting him know he would be at the dorm later and he would be attending class the next day. His mom called Mike and David and invited them to join their lunch celebration. Mike was unable to get away, but he sent his congratulations. David texted he was on his way. Will stood and gave David a big smile when he entered the restaurant.

"Wow," said David, staring at Will's completely healed face and shining eyes. "I can hardly believe it. You are completely healed. If the magic mirror did this, I'm going to start paying more attention to mirrors when I look in them. You never know when your true love will be looking back at you."

"Maybe we can get that reporter to write more about the mirror. The more girls looking in the mirror, the better chance of finding the one meant for you," said Will.

"Now you're talking," said David. "Where can I find this reporter?"

"I don't know," said Will. "Maybe we could look her up through the newspaper."

"Why don't you try finding her when you get to your dorm, let me know what you find out," said David.

Cam and Lucy had been listening to the boys talk back and forth. "Are you sure you want to do this?" asked Cam. "You are going to leave your choice of a life partner to a mirror?"

"The mirror only gives you a chance. It's up to you what you do with the chance," said Will. "Everyone still has free will. The mirror does not force anything on anyone."

"I think it is a fine idea," said Lucy. "Maybe you boys will find some nice girls and start families. I want some grandchildren before I get too old to play with them."

Will and David smiled at their mom. "The mirror only promises true love," said David. "It doesn't promise grandchildren."

"Well," said Lucy with a smile. "You have to start somewhere." The guys all laughed with her and settled in to enjoy their lunch.

After lunch, Cam and Lucy drove Will back to the hospital to see Dr. Drake. They met him coming down the hall, before they had a chance to ask for him. He took one look at Will and smiled. "I understand you went by the museum," he said.

"How did you know?" asked Lucy.

"My wife called me and told me about the mirror," said Dr. Drake. "I'm glad everything is alright with your eyes."

"Do you need to run any tests?" asked Will.

"We can wait until your scheduled appointment," replied Dr. Drake. "I will let Dr. Loren know. She is probably not going to believe your eyes are healed unless she checks them out herself. Just take it easy, and we will see you next week."

"Thanks, Dr. Drake," said Will.

"Don't thank me. I did not heal you. Take good care of the magic mirror while you are working at the museum." Dr. Drake smiled and left to go on his hospital rounds.

Cam and Lucy dropped Will off at his dorm room. Tim was waiting for him when he entered the room. "Your face is healed," said Tim in astonishment.

"I know," said Will smiling. "The magic mirror healed me. My eyes are healed as well."

"The magic mirror healed you," echoed Tim. "How could a mirror heal you?"

"It bathed me in a white light, and when the light went away, I was healed," said Will.

"Wow," said Tim. "When this story gets out, there is going to be a rush of girls wanting to go and look in the mirror."

"Yeah," Will frowned. "I am going to have my hands full protecting the mirror for the next three months."

"Why?" asked Tim.

"I have to spend the next three months working at the museum on weekends. One of my jobs is going to be protecting the magic mirror," said Will.

"Wow," said Tim. "Do you think they would let me work there with you?"

"I don't know. Why do you want to?" asked Will.

"I can't think of a better way to meet a lot of girls," said Tim.

Will and Tim both laughed.

"Have you got my class work? I need to get caught up, so I can return to class tomorrow," said Will.

"Sure, I will get it for you," replied Tim, getting out his books and notes for Will.

Will took the notes and started on the work he had missed.

Tim settled down to do his work. The boys were quiet as they worked to catch up on their class assignments.

The next day, before class, Will and Tim were surrounded in the hall. All of the girls wanted to ask Will questions about the magic mirror. Will tried to explain to them that he did not know how the mirror worked. All he knew was that it worked, and it really was magic. The girls were awed, but they finally let them go since class was about to start.

Alison stood to the side and watched the girls crowd around Will. She did not try to push her way in or draw attention to herself. Will saw her and sent her a smile and a shoulder shrug. She came forward when he headed for class and went in with him and Tim.

The teacher saw them enter. She gave Will a hard stare, then came over to speak to him. "Good morning, Mr. Murdoc. I understand you have had some trouble with your eyesight," stated Mrs. Sorange.

"Yes, Ma'am, but it is all healed, now," said Will.

"Good, did you get your makeup work from Mr. Sorason?"

"Yes, Ma'am, I have it right here." Will took the work he had finished the night before and handed it to Mrs. Sorange.

Mrs. Sorange took Will's work and, with another hard look at him, returned to the front of the class.

Will exchanged a smile with Tim. It would be hard for anyone to understand how bad his situation with his eyes had been. He looked as if nothing had happened. He hoped everyone was not going to be as skeptical as his teacher had been. He did not want them to think he was just making everything up to get out of class. Maybe he needed to get a note from Dr. Drake. Maybe the teachers would take Dr. Drake's word for his injury.

During a free period, Will went to the library and looked up the newspaper article written about the magic mirror. He wanted to get the reporter's name off the byline. He found her name, Janice Slater, and wrote it down. He also wrote down the name and number for the newspaper.

Will went outside and called the paper. He asked to speak to Janice

Slater. The paper said she was out on assignment, so he left his number for her to call him back. The message he left her simply said, "The Magic Mirror Really Works." Will smiled. The message should get her attention.

Evidently, she must have been still out on assignment and did not get his message, because he did not get a call from her that night or the next day.

CHAPTER 5

On Saturday, when Will went in to work at the museum, Valerie was already there. Will knocked on the door and Valerie opened it for him to enter. There was another fifteen minutes until time to open. Valerie took him to the storage room and showed him how to unpack and record new stock.

She explained about having everything unpacked and recorded so it could be placed on the shelves the next day while the store was closed. Valerie left Will unpacking and went out front to open the museum. When Valerie opened the museum, Tim was waiting. He came in and asked Valerie if there was any chance, he could work there on the weekends like Will.

Valerie agreed to give Tim a trial and see how he did.

"If you do a good job, I will see about giving you a more permanent period of employment," explained Valerie.

"Thanks," said Tim. "I promise you won't regret it."

Valerie smiled and showed Tim the room where Will was working. "Will, I brought you some help. Could you explain to Tim about recording the new stock?" she asked.

"Sure, Mrs. Drake, I will be glad to," said Will smiling at Tim.

"I have to get back out front," said Valerie. "If you need anything, one of you can come and let me know."

"Sure, thanks, Mrs. Drake," agreed both boys.

Mid-morning Valerie had another visit from the police. Doug Perkins and Bertha Thorton, the first officers at the scene of the break in, came by to see if she had made up her mind about filing charges against Will. Valerie explained to them about Will working at the museum. She declined to press charges.

"Could we speak with Will?" asked Officer Thorton.

"Sure, I will get him," said Valerie.

"Will." said Valerie sticking her head into the storeroom. "Could you come out front?"

"Sure, Mrs. Drake," responded Will.

Will came into the front room and looked at the two officers curiously. He did not remember them from the night of the break in. "Will, these officers want to speak with you," said Valerie.

Will looked at the officers and smiled.

"What can I do for you?" asked Will.

Officer Bertha Thorton looked at Will. "How did your face heal so fast?" she asked.

Will smiled. "The magic mirror healed it," responded Will.

"How could the magic mirror heal your face? I thought it was just supposed to show girls their true love," she asked.

"I don't know how the mirror healed me. I only know when I apologized for trying to take it, it healed me," said Will.

Officer Thorton went into the next room and stood looking in the mirror. She shook her head. Impossible, she thought. She only saw her own reflection in the mirror.

"You expect us to believe this fantasy?" asked Officer Doug Perkins.

Officer Thorton gave a loud gasp. She was still looking into the mirror when the face of a man appeared in it. She looked behind her, but there was no one there. She looked back at the mirror.

"Who are you?" she demanded.

The man in the mirror grinned at her. "My name is David. Who are you?"

"I am Officer Bertha Thorton. I am with the Denton Police Department," she said.

"You must be at the museum," said David.

"Yes, how did you know?" asked Officer Thorton.

"It is the only place in town that has a magic mirror," said David. "My brother, Will is working there."

"Your brother is Will Murdoc?" asked Officer Thorton.

"Yes," replied David.

"What's going on here? Are you guys trying to pull a fast one?" asked Officer Thorton.

David stopped smiling. "I have nothing to do with who you see in the mirror. The magic mirror does have a mind of its own. It showed us each other for a reason. We are meant to be together."

"Who are you talking to?" asked Officer Perkins. He came into the room and stood looking in the mirror beside Officer Thorton. He could only see his own reflection and Officer Thorton.

Officer Thorton looked at him startled. "You can't see him?" she asked.

"See who?" asked Officer Perkins. "I only see you and me."

"Only you can see me," said David. "Only you can hear me. The magic mirror only lets you see your true love."

Officer Thorton shook her head. "I have to go." She turned away from the mirror and looked at Will. "You have a brother named David?"

"Yes," replied Will. "He and my dad run a car repair shop here in Denton."

She looked at Will for a minute, then turned and left the museum. Officer Perkins hurried to catch up with her.

"What about the break in?" he asked.

"Forget it," she said. "They are not pressing charges." She kept right on going without a pause. It was like she had to get as far away from the mirror as she could.

Officer Perkins followed her out to the car and got in without any more questions. He was a rookie and Officer Thorton was his superior. He shook his head. Something strange had been going on in the museum. It had looked like Officer Thorton had been talking to the mirror. He glanced at her worriedly. He hoped she was alright.

Officer Thorton pulled away from the curve and headed for the police station. She had a lot to think about.

David turned away from the mirror in the bathroom of Murdoc's Auto Repair. He had a big smile on his face. He returned to the shop to continue working on the car he had been repairing before going to the bathroom. Cam looked at David curiously. He was surprised to see him smiling so broadly.

"What's up?" he asked. "I don't think I ever seen anyone so happy to go to the bathroom."

David laughed. "I think I just met my future."

"In the bathroom?" asked Cam.

"In the bathroom mirror," said David with another laugh. "She was looking in the magic mirror at the museum. She is a police officer. Her name is Officer Bertha Thorton."

"What was she doing at the museum?" asked Cam.

"I don't know," said David. "We didn't get to talk long."

"I wonder if it has anything to do with Will," said Cam.

"I tell you I just met the love of my life and all you can think about is Will?" said David.

Cam looked over at David. "I'm sorry," he said. "Your mother and I will look forward to meeting Miss Thorton. Your mother is going to be over the moon with excitement."

"I know," grinned David. "I think she was beginning to think none of us would meet a possible future mate."

"She keeps saying she's not getting any younger," agreed Cam.

Cam and David lay down on their dollies and rolled under the car they were working on.

"When do you think we may be able to meet her?" asked Cam.

"I don't know," said David. "I have to meet her and convince her that the mirror is real, and we are meant to be together. You two are going to have to be patient."

"Yeah, you're right," sighed Cam. "We are going to have to wait."

"If I have my way, you won't have too long a wait," said David.

They concentrated on the car and put the subject of romance aside for the time being. David didn't lose his happy look, even while working.

At the police station, Officer Thorton reported to her Captain. She explained about the museum not pressing charges and about Will working at the museum.

"Fine," said the Captain. "If they don't want to press charges, we move on. We have enough other cases to handle without trying to make a case where there is none."

"Yes, sir," agreed Officer Thorton.

She went to her desk and began filling out paperwork. Officer Perkins stopped at her desk a few minutes later. He had been wandering around, talking to some of his friends among the new recruits.

Officer Thorton glanced up at him and then continued filling out her report.

"The Captain said to close this case," she remarked.

"Okay," agreed Officer Perkins. "What will we be working on next?"

Officer Thorton glanced at her watch, "Nothing today, it's almost quitting time. As soon as I finish this report, I am out of here. I will be able to pick up my son on time for once," she remarked. "We can get a fresh start in the morning."

"Okay," agreed Officer Perkins. "I'll see you in the morning."

"Good night," said officer Thorton. She finished up her paperwork and logged out. She headed for the daycare to pick up the love of her life, her three-year-old son, Amos.

When Amos saw his mother enter the daycare, he put down the toy he was playing with, and leaving his playmates; he got to his feet and ran as fast as his short legs would carry him into his mother's arms.

"Mommy, Mommy," he squealed.

"Hello, Amos," said Bertha. She took him into her arms and held him tightly. "Did you have a good day?" she asked.

"Yes," said Amos nodding his head. "I missed you."

"I missed you, too," replied Bertha, kissing his cheek. Turning, Bertha waved at the daycare worker and took Amos outside. She strapped him into his car seat and headed for home.

"We go to park?" asked Amos as Bertha unfastened him from his car seat and prepared to carry him inside.

"We have to eat first," said Bertha. "If it is still light enough when we finish eating, maybe we can go to the park for a little while."

She carried Amos and gave him some toys to play with while she prepared something to eat. After feeding Amos, Bertha cleaned him and put him in a clean shirt.

Her dad came in as she was getting ready. Amos ran to give his grandpa a hug. Bertha gave her dad a hug, also. "Where are you two off to?" asked Charlie Thorton.

"We go to park," responded Amos. Charlie laughed.

"I'll fix supper when we get back," said Bertha. "We won't stay long."

"Take your time. I'm in no hurry. If I get hungry, I can make a sandwich. Let Amos enjoy the playground," said Charlie.

"Okay, Dad," we will see you soon," said Bertha. "Tell grandpa bye, Amos."

"Bye, Grandpa," responded Amos.

"Bye, Amos, you have fun," ordered Charlie.

Bertha and Amos left and started the short walk to the park. It was only a block away from their house. There was a group of other youngsters and assorted adults already in the park. They were scattered around at different play areas.

Amos headed for the slide. It was his favorite. Bertha helped him to climb up. She then went around to the front to catch him when he came down.

Bertha smiled. She always got a good workout at the park with Amos. It helped her to make up for sitting in the car all day.

David was on his way home. He lived across from the park. He decided to take a stroll around the park. He had some thinking to do.

In the park, Amos was playing toss the ball with a little friend. His friend tossed the ball to him as David walked by. Amos missed the ball and it rolled in front of David. David reached down and picked up the ball and, with a smile, held it out to Amos. With a big grin, Amos took the ball and threw it to his friend. The friend threw it back and Amos missed it again. David caught the ball when Amos missed it. He offered it to Amos with a smile.

"Thanks," said Amos. He was fascinated by the stranger playing ball with him.

David knelt on one knee and prepared to help Amos catch the ball. When the other boy threw the ball again, David helped Amos reach and capture the ball. Amos laughed delightedly.

Bertha had been watching Amos play ball with his little friend. She was shocked when she saw the man from the mirror appear and start playing with Amos. She headed over to Amos.

"Hey, Mom," called Amos, when he spotted his mom approaching.

David looked around with a smile, when Amos spoke. The smile faded when he saw the lady approaching. The lady being called Mom by the little boy he was playing with. David starred at her as she drew close. When she stopped beside him, he smiled at her.

"Are you married?" asked David.

"No," replied Bertha.

"Good," said David.

"Mom, this is my friend," said Amos tugging on his mom's hand to get her attention.

"I can see that," replied Bertha, pulling Amos close to her side.

"David, this is my son, Amos. We were about to head home so I could prepare some food for my dad. Would you like to walk with us? It's not far," stated Bertha.

"I would love to walk with you and Amos," said David.

Amos took David's hand and walked with him as they left the park. Bertha looked on in amazement. Amos was usually very slow to get along with people. He was really taken with David and David seemed to be just as taken with Amos.

While they were walking, David pointed out his house to Bertha and Amos. Bertha was impressed. David's house was larger than theirs'.

"Are you married?" asked Bertha.

"No," replied David. "I've never been married. I've been waiting for you." Bertha looked at him quickly, startled. He certainly believed in plain speaking. "What happened to Amos' father?" asked David softly.

"He died before I even knew Amos was on the way. We were engaged. He and I graduated the police academy at the same time. He was sent out on a call at a bank robbery. He was shot and died instantly."

"I'm sorry," said David softly.

Bertha smiled at him. "Amos was my blessing. He kept me sane. He is a very happy little boy."

"I can see what a joy he is," agreed David. "He and I are going to be great friends. Aren't we, buddy?" David turned to Amos.

Amos smiled happily and turning gave David a big hug. David picked him up and hugged him back. Amos' little arms around his neck felt so right. David smiled at Bertha over Amos' shoulder.

Bertha smiled back at him. "Here we are," said Bertha stopping at their front door. "Would you like to come in and meet my dad?" asked Bertha.

"Yes, I would," agreed David. He walked in behind Bertha as she held the door open for him to enter with Amos still in his arms.

"Is Amos hurt?" asked Charlie. He was startled to see Amos entering in a stranger's arms.

"No," said Bertha. "He is fine. He just felt like being carried."

Charlie looked surprised at this information. His independent grandson usually loves being on his own two feet.

"Dad, this is David Murdoc. David, this is my dad, Charlie Thorton."

"Pleased to meet you, sir," said David, going over and shaking hands, while still holding Amos.

"It is good to meet you, David," replied Charlie. "How did you meet my daughter?"

"She saw me in the magic mirror at the museum," replied David.

"David," exclaimed Bertha turning back from the kitchen when she heard David talking about the magic mirror.

"What?" asked David turning to look at her. "It is the truth."

"I know," she replied. "I don't know if I am ready to talk about the magic mirror."

David shook his head and smiled. "I won't rush you, but you, me and Amos are going to be a family."

"Yes," agreed Amos, sleepily, from David's shoulder.

"Here, let me take him to his bed," said Charlie, taking Amos from David. Amos gave a small protest, then allowed his grandpa to carry him to his bed for a nap.

David followed Bertha into the kitchen. "Is there anything I can help with?" he asked.

"No, you can go into the other room and keep my dad company. No more talking about the magic mirror," she said sternly.

David smiled at her and kissed her on the tip of her nose. They were both surprised when they got a shock from the contact. "Oh, what was that?" asked Bertha.

"I have heard about people being matched by the magic mirror. They get a shock when they touch. It is something to do with the magic," replied David.

"Does it keep on happening?" asked Bertha.

"I don't know," said David. He reached for her hand. When they made contact, there was a shock, but he kept holding her hand and the shock faded.

"Well, I guess the secret is to keep contact. The shock only works when you touch. If you don't let go, you won't get another shock.

David pulled her close and kissed her lightly. He kept her hand in his and did not let go. There was no shock.

"Ummm," said Bertha. "I can see we will have a lot of contact." She smiled at him. "The only problem is, I can't cook with one hand."

"Sure, you can. I'll help. We can use one of your hands and one of mine," said David.

Bertha laughed and pulled her hand away. "You go and talk with Dad. I'll fix supper. Will you stay and eat with us?"

"Sure, I would love to," replied David.

"Go," said Bertha giving him a small nudge.

"Okay," said David in surrender. "I'm going." He turned and went in the other room to join Charlie.

CHAPTER 6

*W*hen David entered the other room, Charlie was already there. He had the television on. He was watching the news.

"Bertha ran me out of the kitchen," said David.

Charlie laughed. "She doesn't like to be bothered when she is cooking," explained Charlie.

"Are you the Murdoc who owns the car repair shop?" asked Charlie.

"Yes, sir, my dad and I run the shop. My brother, Mike is studying to be a veterinarian. He is working as an assistant with the local veterinarian while going to school. My youngest brother, Will, is in college and my mom is a book- keeper at the sewing factory."

"Is Will the one I saw on the news. Something about breaking into the museum and taking the magic mirror," said Charlie.

"Yes, sir, Will was trying to keep his girlfriend from looking in the magic mirror. He was injured at the time, but he is all right now. He is working part-time at the museum to make up for everything," David paused to take a breath.

"You be careful with my daughter and grandson. I don't want either of them hurt," said Charlie.

"I am very serious about both of them. The draw between us is amazing. I felt it with Amos even before I knew he was Bertha's child. I think the magic mirror knew we needed to be a family," said David.

Charlie shook his head. He didn't know what to make about all the talk about the magic mirror. He was a simple man and he always looked for simple explanations about everything. A magic mirror was beyond his comprehension.

"How does the magic mirror work?" asked Charlie.

"I don't know. I only know it works. I was in the bathroom at the shop, I was washing my hands and I looked up into the mirror and I saw Bertha looking back at me. I think she was as startled as I was," said David smiling. "I knew right away she was at the museum, because of all we had gone through with Will. We only got to talk for a minute before the mirror cut us off. Then, after work, I was taking a walk in the park to unwind and think. I bumped into Amos. When I heard him call Bertha mom, my heart was in my throat until she told me she wasn't married. It was a heart stopping moment, but then I could breathe again." David stopped and looked at Charlie.

Charlie was grinning. "Did anyone ever say you should take up writing? You are good at storytelling.

"Just telling the truth, sir," declared David.

"Enough of this, sir. Call me Charlie."

"Sure thing, Charlie," said David.

In the kitchen, while preparing supper, Bertha was listening to her dad and David talk. She couldn't hear everything being said, but she heard enough to learn more about David and his family. It sounded like her dad approved of David. Her dad was very protective of her and Amos. He had been extra protective since Larry died. Bertha didn't know what she would have done if she had not had her dad's help and support during that time while she was dealing with Larry's death and her unexpected pregnancy.

Her dad had been there for her all the way. He adored his grandson and Amos thought the sun rose and set with his grandpa. Bertha smiled. She was glad there was such a good connection between David and Amos. She had never seen her shy little boy take to anyone the way he had David. He was drawn to David as much as she was. Bertha shook her head. She may as well admit it to herself. She was very drawn to David. She had not been drawn to anyone since Larry had died. The feelings she had for David left her breathless. She tingled at his touch and standing next to David made her feel breathless. She felt alive in a way she had not felt in a long time.

Bertha laughed. Score one for the magic mirror. She was so glad she had gone into the room at the museum and gazed into the mirror. Bertha finished putting supper on the table. She looked into the living room and saw David and her dad in a lively discussion about a game show on the television.

"Are you two ready to eat?" she asked with a smile.

"Sure," said David smiling. He stood and smiled at her while her dad turned off the television. "It smells great," said David.

"It's just pot roast. I fixed it this morning. It has been cooking in the slow cooker all day," said Bertha. "I made a salad to go with it."

David followed her into the dining room and held her chair for her to sit. Her dad took his seat at the head of the table and David sat in the chair across from Bertha at Charlie's other side.

"How did things go at work today, Dad?" asked Bertha.

"They were fine, but I will be glad to have Herman back tomorrow," he said.

"Dad works at Grey's hardware," explained Bertha. "Mr. Grey and his wife were on vacation this past week and Dad was in charge."

"I've been in Grey's hardware lots of times," said David. "I don't remember seeing you there," said David puzzled.

"I work in the office most of the time. I help out front if we get crowded. Herman has taken more time off since his sons had married and have started producing some grandchildren for him. I don't blame him. It is a joy to spend time with Amos."

"I know what you mean," said David. "My mom has been asking when we are going to provide her with some grandchildren. She is going to be excited when she learns about Amos."

"Aren't you getting a little ahead of yourself?" asked Bertha with a grin.

"No," declared David, "You and Amos are going to be my family. He will have another grandpa, a grandma, and two uncles. They will all love him, and they will welcome all three of you into our family with open arms."

Bertha and Charlie sat stunned. Charlie had a grin as he turned to look at Bertha to see how she was taking this declaration. Bertha looked at David and then at her dad. She burst out laughing. David and Charlie looked at each other and smiled.

"What's so funny?" Charlie asked.

"I was remembering a saying I heard. It said be careful what you wish for, you just might get it," said Bertha.

"What were you wishing for?" asked Charlie.

"I was wishing Amos had a dad. He was crying a few days ago. Some little girl at daycare told him he should have a dad. He was very upset. He wanted to know why he didn't have a dad like the other kids. I tried to explain about his dad dying, but I don't think he understood," Bertha explained.

David came around the table and drew Bertha into his arms. He held her close for a minute while she composed herself. He looked down into her face and smiled. Charlie watched them with satisfaction.

"When is your next day off," asked David.

"Day after tomorrow," said Bertha. "Why?'

"I want you, Amos and Charlie to have supper at my folks' house. I want you all to meet each other, said David.

Bertha looked at David, then, she looked at Charlie. Charlie shrugged and nodded. "You check with your mom first. I want to be sure it is okay with her. You can call me and let me know what she says," said Bertha.

David smiled in agreement. "I will need your phone number," he agreed.

Bertha held out her hand for his phone. David handed it to her, and she called her number. When her phone rang, she saved David's number in her phone. She gave David's phone back to him.

"I had better go and let you get some rest," David gave her another hug and reluctantly let her go. "I'll see you all, the day after tomorrow. Thanks for supper."

"You're welcome," said Bertha.

Bertha walked him to the door, where he gave her another hug and a gentle kiss before leaving. Bertha leaned against the door after he left. She was gazing into space and smiling.

Charlie looked at Bertha's happy face and smiled as he headed to his bedroom. Things were going to change. He thought to himself. It should be a happy change for his small family.

While David was walking home, he took out his phone and made sure Bertha's number was saved in his phone. He then called his mom.

"Mom, I have met the love of my life, her name is Bertha. She has a little boy, Amos. He is three years old. I invited her, her dad, Charlie, and Amos to supper in two days. Bertha insisted I call you to be sure it was alright before she agreed," said David.

"Of course, it is alright. Your dad had already told me about someone seeing you in the magic mirror. How did you get together so quickly?" asked Lucy.

"I bumped into Bertha and Amos in the park. Amos and I were playing ball and Bertha and I recognized each other. I walked them home and met, Charlie Thorton, her dad. I stayed for supper and we all talked. We got to know each other a little better."

"Your dad said Bertha is a policewoman. What does her dad do?" asked Lucy.

"He works at Grey's hardware store," replied David. David arrived at his house and went inside while still talking to his mom. "I'm home now. I will talk to you later. I need to call Bertha and let her know you are okay with supper. Good night, Mom, love you."

"Good night, David. I love you, too." David quickly dialed Bertha's number. He smiled when she answered on the first ring.

"Hello," said Bertha.

"Hello, beautiful," said David. "I talked to my mom. She is excited about meeting you and Amos. She said she would be happy to have all of you to supper day after tomorrow."

"You didn't waste any time," said Bertha with a smile.

"I don't waste time when something is this important to me," said David seriously. "I want everyone to meet you and Amos. I want them to know how important you both are to me."

"Oh, David," Bertha was all choked up with emotion.

"I know we just met, but we are meant to be a family. The magic mirror doesn't make mistakes. I felt our connection, even though the mirror, the first time I looked into your eyes," David said softly.

"I know. I felt it too," said Bertha, "I will never have anything bad to say about the magic mirror again. I didn't really believe in magic, but I will always be a believer, now."

"Yes, I will have to give my brother a big thank you for trying to keep his girl away from the magic mirror. I refuse to believe we would not have met anyway, but the mirror sure speeds things up," declared David.

"Yes, it did," agreed Bertha. "I have to go and try to get some sleep. I have to work tomorrow."

"Yeah, me too," agreed David. "Sleep well, dream of us. I love you."

"Good night," said Bertha as she hung up. There was a big, dreamy smile on her face.

David hung up and went to shower before lying down and thinking about all of his daily happenings. It had been a very eventful day. He smiled happily. Life was an adventure. He could not wait to start exploring this adventure with Bertha and Amos. He settled in to dream the night away.

The next morning, as soon as he had sent Bertha a good morning text, David called Will.

"Hello," said Will sleepily.

"Hello, Will," said David cheerfully.

"David, why are you calling so early? Is something wrong?" Will was becoming more alert.

"No, nothing is wrong. Something is very right. I called to thank you," said David.

"Thank me," said Will puzzled. "Thank me for what?"

"I want to thank you for going after the magic mirror. Because of you, I have met the love of my life. The magic mirror said so," said David chuckling.

"The magic mirror showed you your true love!" exclaimed Will.

"Well the magic mirror showed her, but it wouldn't have happened without you," said David.

"What did I have to do with it?" asked Will.

"If you had not tried to take the mirror, the police would not have been at the museum and Bertha would not have looked in the mirror," said David.

"You mean Officer Thorton is your true love!" exclaimed Will.

"Yes, and we are going to have supper at Mom and Dads' tomorrow night so everyone can meet Bertha and her family. I'll expect you to be there," said David firmly.

"Okay," said Will. He hung up the phone and looked around. "Things sure do happen quickly around here," he said.

He looked over and saw Tim grinning at him. He had been awakened by the phone and had listened to Will's side of the conversation. "You are going to have a sister-in-law," he said.

"It looks that way," agreed Will. "We are going to have a police officer in the family. I guess I will have to make sure not to do anything foolish again."

Tim laughed. "She seemed like a nice lady."

"Yes," agreed Will. "Well, since we are awake, we might as well go eat and get ready for church and then work." Tim agreed and they both got ready to start their day.

Bertha read the text from David and, with a smile, she texted him back. She added a smiley face to the message. Laughing she went to get Amos up and fed so she could go to work.

In the kitchen, Bertha found the coffee already made. She poured herself a cup, and after taking a big swallow, started preparing breakfast for Amos and herself. She made oatmeal and raisins for them both, glad Amos liked oatmeal and raisins as much as she did. It was one of her favorite breakfast meals.

"Come on sleepy head," said Bertha as she roused Amos from a very sound sleep.

"Is it time to get up?" asked Amos sleepily.

"Yes, I have breakfast ready. I made oatmeal," said Bertha.

"With raisins?" asked Amos.

"Of course, with raisins," declared Bertha.

Amos reached his arms around his mom's neck and hugged her when she bent toward him.

"I love you, Mom," he said.

"I love you, too," said Bertha, giving him an extra hug.

Amos hurried into his clothes, with a little help from Bertha, and headed for the table and his waiting bowl of oatmeal.

"Is David going to be here today?" asked Amos.

"I don't know about today, but we are going to his family's house for supper tomorrow night," replied Bertha with a smile. Amos gave a big, satisfied smile. Bertha looked at him curiously. "You like David, don't you?" she asked.

"Yes," said Amos, nodding his head. "He likes me, too."

"Yes, he does," agreed Bertha.

They finished eating and Bertha rinsed their bowls and put them in the dishwasher. She then gathered all the things she had to take with her and helped Amos into his car seat. She shook her head and headed for daycare. "Another day in the life of a single mom," she thought.

CHAPTER 7

*C*am was in his office when David entered the repair shop on Monday morning. He smiled with satisfaction when he saw how happy David looked. All he wanted for his boys was for them to have happy, fulfilled lives.

"Morning, Dad," said David.

"Good morning," said Cam. "Your mom is very excited about tonight. She is looking forward to meeting Bertha and her family."

"I know," said David. "She is going to be even more excited when she meets Amos. He is a sweetheart."

"I think you have hit the jackpot," said Cam.

"Yes, I did," said David with satisfaction. The two of them went into the shop to begin their day's work.

Lucy had taken the day off at the sewing factory, so she could prepare for visitors. She sat down and worked on a menu and made a list of things she needed. After she was sure she had covered everything, she grabbed her purse and headed for the grocery store. She made quick work of getting everything on her lists. After she had put everything away at home, she went to the attic and pulled out a box with some of her boys' old toys. There were a lot of cars and soldiers in the box, along with some building toys.

Lucy carried the toys downstairs and set them in the corner of the living room. She smiled with happiness. It would be great to see the toys played with again.

Lucy went into the kitchen and gathered the dishes and utensils she would need for supper and laid them on the counter. She decided not to put a cloth on the table. She found a nice center piece and put it in the middle of the table. She then proceeded to set the table. When she had everything arranged to her satisfaction, she went into the living room and looked around to see if anything needed cleaning. It all looked good, so she sat down to try to relax for a while.

Meanwhile, Beth had persuaded Alison to go to the museum with her during their free period. Beth wanted Alison to look in the magic mirror. Beth was determined to see if Will was Alison's true love.

The girls went into the museum and looked around. They did not see the mirror. There was a young woman working there who came over to see if she could help them.

"We wanted to see the magic mirror," said Beth.

"It is in the next room. My name is Sarah. I work here part-time. I am going to college. I think I have seen you around campus," she said to Beth as she led them to the next room.

"I am going to college, but I don't remember seeing you there," said Beth.

"You probably wouldn't," replied Sarah. "This is my first year. The mirror is over here." Sarah led them over to where the mirror was displayed. It still had a chair in front of it. The chair had been put in place for Will to use.

Beth urged Alison to sit in the chair. Alison sat in the chair and looked in the mirror. Nothing happened. Alison looked up at Sarah and shook her head.

"I only see myself," she said.

"Your true love may not be around a reflective surface," replied Sarah.

"Oh," said Alison. "You mean I cannot see him if he is not where the mirror can show him," said Alison.

"Yes, the mirror has to be able to show a reflection," agreed Sarah.

Alison rose from the chair. After she moved aside, Beth sat in the chair. Beth looked in the mirror. She caught a glimpse of someone going out of a bathroom door. The figure was gone so fast, she could not tell who it was. The mirror cleared and all Beth could see was herself.

"There was someone, but I couldn't tell who it was," she said standing and looking at Sarah and Alison.

Sarah smiled. "You will have to come and try again sometime."

"Yes, we both will," agreed Beth. "I have caught a glimpse and I won't be satisfied until I see who the mirror has picked for my true love."

"We will both be back as soon as we can," agreed Alison.

"You might have better luck around lunch time or in the evening after class finishes," said Sarah.

"You may be right," agreed Alison. "Thanks for showing us the mirror."

"You are welcome. I was happy to do it. It can get boring around here sometimes. I was glad to talk with fellow students," said Sarah.

"Have you looked in the magic mirror?" asked Beth.

"Yes, but I did not see anyone. I guess I will have to keep trying," said Sarah.

"Good luck," said Beth with a smile as she and Alison Left.

"Thank you," replied Sarah giving them a small wave.

Will was leaving his last class of the day when he received a phone call.

"Hello," answered Will.

"This is Janice Slater; I received a message from you, something about the magic mirror. I have been away on an assignment and I have just returned."

"Yes, my name is Will Murdoc. I wanted to see if you were interested in doing a follow-up story on the magic mirror."

"Do you have any new information for me?" asked Janice.

"Yes, I was trying to keep my girlfriend from looking in the magic mirror. I dropped the mirror and it broke into two pieces. Two streaks of light came from the mirror and struck me in the face. I had blisters and redness on my face and could only see blurs. When I got out of the hospital I went and apologized to the mirror. The mirror then healed my face and my eyesight. Another thing about the mirror, even though it broke into two pieces, it was one piece again when the police arrived. The police don't believe it was broken, but it was."

"It sounds like you have a good follow up story," said Janice. "Which one of the magic mirrors were you looking into?"

"I was at the museum in Denton," explained Will.

"I will be in Denton on Thursday. Would you be able to meet and talk to me?" asked Janice.

"I have class, but if you will give me a call when you arrive, I'll meet you and we can talk," agreed Will.

"I'll see you on Thursday," said Janice.

Will hung up and turned to Tim.

"The newspaper lady, Janice Slater is going to be here on Thursday to do a follow-up story on the magic mirror," he said. "With any luck the additional publicity will bring in more girls to look in the mirror. Maybe you and Mike will be lucky enough to find your true loves."

"Whether we find true love or not, we should have a lot of girls coming to town," said Tim rubbing his hands together with satisfaction.

David had a car seat fitted in his car for Amos. He went by the Thorton home to pick up Bertha, Charlie and Amos to take them to his parents for supper. Bertha started to tell him they could take their own car because of the car seat.

"I have a car seat in my car," replied David. "I had it installed today."

"You had a car seat installed?" asked Bertha surprised.

"Of course," declared David. "Amos is part of my family, now. I am in this for the long haul."

He drew Bertha close and gave her a hug and a quick kiss. He looked down at Amos, who was watching them with a huge grin on his face.

"Hi," said David, picking Amos up and giving him a hug, too. "Are you ready to meet your new grandparents?"

Amos nodded happily. Charlie was just watching them all. He was not trying to influence anyone. He was happily going along and letting everyone decide for themselves, but he had a happy, relaxed look about him.

David led the way to his car and strapped Amos into his new car seat. Charlie climbed into the back seat with Amos and David held the front door open for Bertha to sit beside him. Bertha smiled at him and took her seat. While Bertha fastened her seat belt, David went around the car and took the driver's seat.

Cam and Lucy lived on the outskirts of town. Their place was once almost all country, but the town had grown until it caught up and passed them. They still enjoyed the semi country area. They had a large fenced yard. The boys had really enjoyed growing up there. There was an old tire swing in the yard along with a more conventional style play set. There was a tree house in the large oak tree. Cam and the boys had built it one summer when the boys were just beginning their teen years.

Bertha looked around in amazement as David turned in and drove up the drive to the house. Cam was sitting in the porch swing on the wrap around porch. He rose and came forward to greet them. David helped Bertha out and then turned to get Amos. Charlie exited the car and headed over to greet Cam.

Cam stuck his hand out to shake Charlie's.

"I'm Charlie Thorton."

"I'm Cam Murdoc," said Cam. "I've seen you at the hardware store. David said you worked there."

"Yes, I work mostly in the office, but I help out in the store sometimes," said Charlie.

Lucy came out on the porch. She had heard Cam talking and decided to see if David's guests had arrived.

Cam took her hand and drew her over to be introduced to Charlie. David and Bertha were on their way to the porch. David was carrying Amos and had an arm around Bertha. Lucy beamed at the group. Amos shyly kept his face hidden close to David.

"Mom, Dad this is Bertha. Bertha, these are my parents, Lucy and Cam Murdoc." They all greeted each other and then looked at Amos.

"This little guy is Amos."

"Hello, Amos," said Lucy smiling up at Amos. "Would you like to come with Nana and see what I have in the living room?"

Amos looked at David and then back at Lucy. He nodded his head shyly. David let him down and he shyly took Lucy's outstretched hand and let her lead him inside. Lucy took him over to the box of toys, she had put there earlier. Amos looked up at her with a big grin.

"Go ahead," she said. "You can play with them. David once played with them when he was a small boy like you."

Amos looked over at David. The rest of the group had followed Amos and Lucy inside. David joined them and looked in the box.

"I haven't seen these in a long time," he said, pulling out some soldiers and handing them to Amos. Amos took them with a big smile and started playing. David stayed with him for a couple of minutes. Then, he rose and went to make sure all was okay with Bertha and his parents.

They had only just begun talking, when Will rapped on the door and entered.

"Hi, everyone," said Will. "It's nice to see you again Officer Thorton."

"Please, it's, Bertha, I'm not Officer Thorton tonight. This is my dad, Charlie and my son, Amos."

Will came forward and shook hands with Bertha and Charlie.

"Hi, Amos," he called to Amos.

Amos looked up and said hi and went back to playing. He was lining the soldiers up beside the box.

Lucy and Bertha left to see to supper. Cam and Charlie had taken a seat and were talking quietly.

Will and David went over and sat on the floor and started playing with Amos and the soldiers. Amos grinned at them. He was pleased to have them show him so much attention.

Mike came in and said hello to Cam and Charlie. He then headed over to get down and play with Amos and his group. Lucy and Bertha looked into the living room. They were about to call everyone to eat, but they looked over at the guys and Amos playing and laughed.

"When I brought those toys down, I was getting them for Amos to play with," said Lucy. "I had no idea you guys were going to revert to childhood."

Mike got up and went over to give his mom a hug. "Ah, Mom, you know we can't resist the lure of all those memories."

"I know. Why don't you guys help Amos wash his hands while you wash your own? Supper is ready," she said. Bertha laughed. "If they are going to act like small children, I am going to treat them like small children," stated Lucy.

David picked Amos up and headed toward the bathroom. He came by Bertha, and leaning down, gave her a quick kiss. Amos was smiling at them.

Lucy had Cam get down a booster seat earlier and clean it up for Amos. David put Amos in his booster chair between him and Bertha.

Lucy had made fried chicken, but she had made some small pieces, without bones, for Amos. They had mashed potatoes and green beans. There was also a large fruit salad. Bertha was fixing Amos his plate. Every time she asked him if he wanted anything, he would glance at David's plate. If David had the food on his plate, Amos nodded his head. Bertha exchanged a look with David. David was pleased to see Amos copying him. He was going to have to watch his actions and be a good role model for Amos.

"I had a call from Janice Slater today," said Will.

"Who is Janice Slater?" inquired Cam.

"She is the reporter who wrote the articles about the magic mirror," said Will.

"What did she want?" asked Lucy.

"She wants to talk to me and maybe write another article on the magic mirror," said Will. "She is going to be in town on Thursday."

"Do you think it is a good idea to talk to her about the mirror?" asked Lucy.

Will shrugged. "I can't see where it would hurt. It will probably draw more girls into look in the mirror. Maybe one of them will see Mike." Will looked at Mike and grinned.

"I'm all for more girls in town," agreed Mike.

"I hope you don't regret it," said Lucy.

"I did see David in the mirror, so I can tell you it works," said Bertha. She looked at David and smiled.

"Tim is looking forward to having a larger group of girls looking in the mirror," said Will.

"What about you?" David asked. "Are you still hung up on Alison or are you open for another relationship?"

"I don't know about Alison. Things have changed between us since my hospital stay. I don't know if I need to be in a relationship with someone who causes me to act in such a way. I need to know my love is true and returned," Will looked down at the table as he finished talking.

"You're both young. You have plenty of time. Don't rush into anything," said Lucy.

Bertha flushed and looked at David. David shook his head at her. "She is not talking about us. We have the magic mirror's blessing. I love you and Amos, and we are going to be a family," insisted David.

Lucy shook her head. "I was not talking about you and David. I am very happy you two found each other and I am glad you, Amos and Charlie are going to be a part of our family."

Bertha looked around the table. Her eyes were glistening with unshed tears. "Thank you all for such a warm welcome," she said.

"Remember we are here for you," said Cam. "You need anything, you let us know. Even if it is only to get your car fixed, just let us know."

Everyone laughed at this last statement. The atmosphere was lightened considerably.

CHAPTER 8

*B*y the time Thursday arrived, Will was getting nervous about talking to Janice about the magic mirror. He was wondering what the mirror would think about him talking about it. He decided to ask the mirror before he talked to Janice.

Will had a free period during the morning, so he headed to the museum to see if he could find out what the mirror felt about publicity.

Valerie was in the front room when he went into the museum. "Hi, Will, you aren't supposed to work, today are you?" asked Valerie.

"No, Ma'am, I was wondering if I could ask the magic mirror a question," said Will.

"I don't see why not," said Valerie with a shrug.

Will went into the room with the mirror and sat in the chair.

"I don't know if I will get an answer, but I thought I should ask before talking to the reporter about you," said Will. "She wants to write a story about all the magic mirrors. She wants to bring you to the attention of more girls. I do not know if this is okay with you, but I thought I should ask."

Will sat quietly in front of the mirror after asking its opinion. Nothing happened for a minute, then, the mirror flashed as if a light had been turned on then off. Will smiled. The magic mirror was okay with him talking with Janice.

Valerie was waiting when Will finished talking to the magic mirror and started to leave. He had a satisfied smile on his face. "I think the magic mirror likes you," she said. "I have not heard of them having any interaction with anyone else."

"I respect it and it respects me," said Will. "At least it let me know it is okay to talk to a reporter."

"When is she going to be here?" asked Valerie.

"She will be in town this evening. I don't know when she will get by the museum," said Will. "I have to hurry. I am between classes. Thanks for letting me talk to the magic mirror."

"You are welcome. The mirror is on display. You can see it anytime," responded Valerie.

Will smiled, and with another thank you, hurried back to the college. He bumped into Tim as he headed for his next class. Tim walked beside him into the room.

"I asked the magic mirror if it was okay to talk to a reporter about it. The magic mirror is okay with it. I guess it wants to help more girls find their true love," said Will.

"How do you know it is okay with the reporter?" asked Tim.

"I just know," said Will. "The magic mirror gets its feelings across."

"Do you mind if I come with you when you talk to the reporter?" asked Tim.

Will smiled. "I was hoping you would. She is supposed to call me and let me know where to meet her. I'll have to let you know our plans later."

"Okay," agreed Tim. He quickly turned his attention to his class as the teacher entered the room.

Janice called as he and Tim were leaving their last class of the day. They had left the building and were on the way to their dorm when Will's phone rang.

"Hello," answered Will.

"Hello, Will, this is Janice Slater. I am at the coffee shop across from Grey's bakery. Are you ready to meet?"

"Yes, I am out of class. We will be there shortly," said Will. He hung up his phone and turned to Tim. "Janice Slater is here. She is at the coffee shop across from Grey's bakery. I told her we would be right there," said Will

"Let's go," said Tim.

The guys hurried on to the dorm to pick up Will's car. They were soon on their way to meet Janice. Both were excited, but a little apprehensive. It wasn't every day they would be interviewed by a famous reporter.

It wasn't hard to spot Janice when they entered the coffee shop. She was older than most of the customers, and she had her nose stuck in a tablet. She was not paying any attention to anyone around her. Will walked up to her table. "Miss Slater?" he asked.

Janice looked up with a smile. "Yes, you must be Will Murdoc," she said.

"Yes, this is my friend Tim Sorason. I hope you don't mind him joining us."

"It is fine," said Janice. She waved her hand. "Why don't you two have a seat and tell me about the mirror."

Will and Tim sat across from Janice. Will took a deep breath and prepared to tell his story. "This all started when my girlfriend decided to go and look in the magic mirror. She said she wanted to see if we were destined to be together. I thought if I could keep her from looking in the mirror, she would forget all about it. I was not thinking straight. I had a skeleton key. It fit the front door of the museum. I thought if I could hide the mirror for a while, I could put it back after Alison had forgotten about it." Will paused to take a breath. Janice was following his story with fascination.

"What happened then?" she asked.

"I must have set off a silent alarm. When I started to leave with the magic mirror, I heard police sirens outside. I was so startled; I dropped the mirror. It broke in half. When it broke, a stream of light shot out from each piece and struck me in the face. Tim had tried to talk me out of taking the mirror, but I wasn't listening. He was outside the museum, and he saw the mirror break. There was so much going on; he didn't see what happened afterwards."

"The doctor said it was like being struck by lightning. I had burns and blisters on my face. My eyes were affected also. My vision was very blurry. After I was taken to the hospital, the police looked at the mirror. It was in one piece again."

"How did it do that?" asked Janice.

"I don't know. I only know it was broken and then it wasn't."

"The doctors didn't know if I was going to get all of my sight back. While I was in the hospital, Mrs. Drake, the museum curator came by to see me. I apologized for breaking into the museum and asked if I could apologize to the magic mirror. Mrs. Drake accepted my apology and said for me to come by the museum after I was discharged from the hospital. She said I could apologize to the magic mirror. If it accepted my apology, they would not press charges for me breaking into the museum."

"How could the magic mirror accept your apology?" asked Janice.

"I wondered that, too. But when I was released from the hospital, my parents took me by the museum. I sat and apologized to the mirror. I told it I was sorry for trying to stop it from doing its job. The mirror bathed my face in a white light. When the light faded, my face was healed, and my sight was restored. Mrs. Drake said I could work weekends to make up for breaking in. She said since the magic mirror had accepted my apology, they were not going to press charges. She also told me that all of the locks at the museum had been changed so the skeleton keys would no longer open the museum door." Will finished his tale and sat back to see what Janice would say.

Janice looked at him thoughtfully. "You had quite an adventure. Are you and your girlfriend still together?"

"I don't know," said Will. "We are still working on our relationship."

"Okay," said Janice. "I will be around town for a few days. I want to go by the museum and I also want to talk to some of the girls who are looking in the magic mirror. I may want to talk to you again. It was nice to meet you both. Thanks for bringing this story to my attention." She held out her hand and shook theirs.

"You are welcome," said Will. "I asked the magic mirror if it was okay to tell you my story. It was fine with it," said Will.

Janice shook her head. "How did it let you know it was okay with you telling your story?"

"It flashed a soft light, like a flashlight going on and off," said Will.

"Okay," said Janice. "I have got to see this magic mirror."

They all left the coffee shop. The guys headed for their dorm and Janice for her motel.

David texted Bertha and asked if she and Amos would like to meet at the park after work. She replied with a yes and a smiley face. She had such a wide smile on her face, her partner, Doug, looked at her curiously. He was not used to seeing Bertha look so happy.

"What's going on?" asked Doug.

"What do you mean?" asked Bertha glancing at him.

"I mean, why do you have a perpetual smile on your face? Have you met someone?"

"Yes, I have," said Bertha with satisfaction.

"Who is he?" asked Doug.

"His name is David Murdoc. He runs Murdoc auto repair with his father," replied Bertha.

"I know him. He worked on a car for my brother. He is a good guy," said Doug.

"Yes, he is," agreed Bertha.

"How did Amos take having a guy around?" asked Doug.

"Amos adores David. David and Amos already have a special relationship," said Bertha.

"I'm happy for you." Doug stopped and thought for a minute. "Is he the guy you saw in the magic mirror?"

"Yes, he is," agreed Bertha with a smile.

Doug sighed. "I wish the magic mirror would send someone my way."

"Are you ready to stop playing the field and settle down?" asked Bertha giving him a curious look.

"I think it would be nice to have someone beside my parents to come home to after work. Someone who would put me first and be there when I turn over at night and want someone to snuggle up to," Doug looked out the window and sighed.

The radio came to life and they listened to the voice telling them to respond to a domestic dispute. They shut off their cares and responded to the call.

~

When David finished work, he made a quick stop at home for a shower, then headed for the park. He spotted Bertha and Amos shortly after entering the park. He started walking toward Bertha. She had her back to him and did not see him coming. Bertha was paying attention to Amos as he played in the sandbox. David came up behind her and put his arms around her.

She jumped, but when she looked over her shoulder and saw David grinning at her, she turned and raised her face for a kiss. David was happy to oblige. Amos glanced at his mom and spotted David. He hurried out of the sandbox and ran toward David and his mom.

He ran up to David and put his arms around David's legs. David reached down and lifted Amos up between the two of them. "How are you doing today, big fellow?" he inquired.

Amos put his sandy hands around David's neck and squeezed tight. "You came," he whispered.

"Of course, I came. I had to see my family," responded David. Amos looked up into his face and smiled. Bertha leaned in close and hugged them both. "How about we take Amos out for ice cream?" asked David.

"I don't know," said Bertha. "Do you want to go out for ice cream?"

"Yes," said Amos nodding emphatically.

"We can walk over to my house and get my car," said David.

"Okay," agreed Bertha.

They started walking out of the park and across to David's house. David carried Amos and guided Bertha with an arm around her, holding her close to his side.

When they arrived downtown, Amos decided he would rather have an Icee. They stopped at a street vendor and picked up a child-sized Icee for each of them. Amos and David got blue ones and Bertha had a red one. They walked over to the downtown park and sat on a bench to eat and enjoy their treats. When they finished them, they threw the cups and napkins into a trash can and headed for David's car for the trip home.

David was not ready to call it an evening, so he stopped at his house instead of taking them to their house. He turned and smiled at Bertha. "You don't mind stopping here, do you? We can see what we can find to eat and if we can't find anything we like, we can order something," he said.

"I think it is a great idea," said Bertha, softly.

David hurried around to help Bertha out of the car and Amos out of his seat. He put Amos down and held out a hand to him. Amos took David's hand and reached for his mom's hand. They went up the steps to the porch. Amos let go and went to sit in the porch swing. Bertha followed him over and sat beside him. David unlocked his front door and joined them in the swing.

Amos smiled at David and nestled up to him. David smiled at Bertha over Amos' head and lay a hand on her shoulder. They sat back, swinging slowly, enjoying the quiet.

David took Bertha's hand and smiled at her. "I know we haven't known each other for very long, but I love you and Amos. I want us to be a family. I want to be your husband and Amos' dad," he looked down at Amos. "Are you okay with me being your dad?" he asked.

Amos nodded enthusiastically. David looked back up and gazed into Bertha's eyes. "Will you be my wife and make us a family?" he asked.

Both David and Amos gazed at Bertha, waiting for her response. Bertha smiled through her tears and nodded. "Yes," she whispered. "I love you, too."

David rose and pulled her into his arms. He kissed her soundly. Amos kept swinging with a big smile on his face. David looked down at Amos. He reached down; and taking him into his arms, included him in the hug with Bertha.

"Wait a minute," said David suddenly. He started walking toward his front door, taking Bertha and Amos along with him. When he got inside, he stood Amos down and turned toward the bookcase in his living room. David looked up on a shelf and found a small box. Taking the box, he turned to Bertha.

"I found this in an antique shop. When I saw it, I knew I had to buy it. When I met you, I knew why I had to buy it. This ring was meant for you," David opened the box and showed the ring to Bertha.

Bertha gasped. It was the most beautiful ring she had ever seen. It had a large emerald surrounded by small diamonds in an antique gold setting.

"It's beautiful," she said holding her hand out for David to put the ring on her finger.

David slipped the ring onto her finger. He kissed her hand and then he pulled her close and kissed her more passionately. When they parted, they both looked down at Amos; he was happily waiting for their attention.

"How do you feel about ordering a pizza?" asked David. Amos nodded and Bertha laughed. "We will have pizza tonight, but tomorrow night, if Charlie will baby sit, we will go out and celebrate our engagement," said David.

"Okay," agreed Bertha. "We haven't discussed where we are going to live."

"I thought you and Amos could move in here. There is more room, and we are close enough to keep an eye on Charlie," said David. "We also have plenty of room for more kids if we decide to have them."

"Kids, how many were you thinking about?" asked Bertha.

"One or two," said David. "I'm not worried about it. If it happens, fine. If it doesn't, we have Amos and each other."

"Do you mind if I keep working?" asked Bertha.

"It's entirely up to you. I make a good amount of money and have a nice savings and a trust fund. I can take care of you both and any future additions, but if you want to work, I have no objections." Bertha snuggled up close and hugged him tightly. She sniffed slightly. David leaned back and looked at her. "Hey, you are not crying, are you?"

"No, I am just so happy. I am afraid I'm going to wake up and find this has all been a dream," she said.

David pulled her close. "If this is a dream, I'm dreaming right along with you and we brought Amos along for the ride. Let's order our pizza before Amos falls asleep on us," said David. They looked over to see Amos sitting on the sofa with his eyelids drooping.

"Yes," agreed Bertha.

David went to his phone and ordered a pizza. He then called Charlie to let him know Bertha and Amos would be home later.

"Thank you for calling Dad," said Bertha. "So much has been going on, I forgot."

"You are welcome. Let's keep Amos occupied so he doesn't fall asleep before the pizza arrives," said David.

They went over and sat down with Amos and started playing with him to keep him awake. David sighed. He couldn't believe how lucky he was. It all started with a magic mirror. Bertha looked at him and smiled. She was having similar thoughts. She blessed the day she had sat down in front of the magic mirror.

CHAPTER 9

*J*anice spoke to several girls around town. She talked to the waitress at the restaurant where she ate. She talked to the girl behind the counter at the drug store, and she talked to the girl at the desk when she checked into the motel. They all had good things to say about the magic mirror. She picked up some names of girls claiming to have seen their true love with its help.

She decided to go by the museum and check out the magic mirror for herself. She had looked into the mirror in Sharpville, but she had not looked into this one. She decided to go by and look around without warning first. She wanted to see the magic mirror before they knew she was a reporter.

There were some people inside the museum when she entered. They glanced her way but then turned back to wandering around. Janice looked but she did not see the magic mirror. She started walking, looking at the displays. After she made her way around the room, she went into the next room. Janice smiled. She spotted the mirror. It was prominently displayed.

Janice did not want to head straight for the magic mirror, so she looked around as she made her way toward it. Several girls looked in the mirror. Most of them turned away, disappointed. One girl squealed and looked closely at the mirror. She joined her friends with a happy expression on her face. They joined hands with her and drew her away. They were excitedly asking her questions about who she had seen in the magic mirror.

The girl shook her head. I am not saying a word until I talk to him. I do not want to jinx myself. The girls kept after her, but she was adamant. Her guy had to be the first to know. The girls departed and Janice made her way over to the magic mirror. She sat down in the chair and looked in the mirror.

"Okay magic mirror; I know I have been skeptical, but I do believe in your magic. I have seen too many of your miracles not to believe. I don't know if there is anyone out there for me, but I figure it can't hurt to ask."

Janice stopped talking and watched in amazement as the magic mirror started to change. As she continued to stare into the mirror, she saw a doctor's office appear. There was a mirror over a washbasin in the patient's exam room. There was a man in a white coat washing his hands. He looked up at the mirror as he was drying his hands. He started smiling.

"Well, hello, who are you?" he asked. He did not seem surprised at all to see someone in his mirror, someone who was not in the room with him.

"I'm Janice Slater. Who are you?" she asked.

"Janice Slater, the reporter?" he asked, as he quit smiling.

"Yes, do you know me?" she asked.

"No," he said shaking his head. "I'm Mike Murdoc. You talked to my brother Will Murdoc."

"Oh, so you already know about the magic mirror. I was wondering why you weren't surprised," said Janice.

"I never expected to see you in my mirror," said Mike.

"Are you a doctor?" asked Janice.

"No, I am a veterinarian assistant. I am studying to be a veterinarian," said Mike.

"I wasn't expecting this," said Janice.

"When you look in the magic mirror you have to expect anything," said Mike.

"I guess so," agreed Janice.

"Will you go out for a meal with me after work?" asked Mike.

"Okay, we have to meet. The magic mirror might be upset if we ignore it," said Janice.

"We sure don't want to make the magic mirror mad," agreed Mike.

"No. we don't," agreed Janice.

"I'll see you in about an hour. Where do you want to meet?" asked Mike.

"I'm at the motel on State. I'm in room sixteen," said Janice.

"I'll be there," said Mike.

The mirror went blank and Janice sat there for a minute just thinking.

Mike went out to the desk and left instructions for the puppy he had been taking care of. He then changed out of his white coat and left the clinic. He was excited to meet someone, but there were going to be complications because she was a reporter and she did not live in Denton. He had not expected this when he talked about meeting someone through the magic mirror.

Mike went by his parent's house and took a shower and changed before heading to town to meet Janice. When Mike knocked on the door to Janice's motel room, she did not keep him waiting. Janice opened the door and smiled up at Mike.

"Hi," said Mike.

"Hi," said Janice.

Mike held out his hand and Janice put her hand in his. "Ouch," exclaimed Janice.

Mike was shaking his hand also. "It's the magic mirror. Whenever it shows anyone in the mirror, they get a shock when they touch," replied Mike.

"Does it get better?' asked Janice.

"I think the shock gets less. It may just be people get used to it," said Mike.

Janice shook her head. "It is a strong shock. It has to tone down eventually."

"Maybe, are you ready to eat?" asked Mike. "I called and made reservations at Marshal's on the way here."

"Sure, I'm ready," said Janice. She reached for her purse and checked to be sure her door was locked.

Mike took her arm to show her to his car. He made sure to only touch where there was sleeve between his hand and her arm. David opened his car door and waited for Janice to get in before closing the door and going to his side to get into the driver's seat. It was not far to Marshal's. He found a parking spot and escorted her inside.

The greeter took them straight to a table. She left them with menus and went to get their drinks.

"Do you know what you would like," asked Mike.

"I think I'll get the seafood salad," said Janice.

"It looks good. I think I'll have it, also," agreed Mike.

The waitress came back with their drinks and took their orders. After she left, Mike looked at Janice and smiled.

"When I was joking with Will about someone seeing me in the magic mirror, I never thought it would actually happen," he confessed,

"I know how you feel. I wrote the story about the magic mirror in Sharpville. I witnessed the miracles it performed. I still never thought it would show me anyone," said Janice.

"It sure changed the lives in my family," said Mike.

"Has someone in your family besides Will been affected?" asked Janice.

"Yeah," Mike grinned. "My brother David, he met the love of his life through the mirror. She was one of the police officers investigating the break-in at the museum. When she looked in the mirror, she saw David. She has a three-year-old son. David is in love with both of them, and Amos thinks of David as his dad already."

Janice smiled at Mike. "It sounds like the magic mirror really likes your family."

Mike grinned back at her. "I have no complaints."

"So, you are studying to be a veterinarian," said Janice.

"Yes, I am almost finished. I have to take my finals. Dr. Long has suggested I join his practice. He is getting older and would like to work shorter hours. I am living at home with my folks until I finish my tests. I have been looking around to see what is available in housing, so I can get my own place. I did not see any need until I finished my studies."

"Will you be able to buy into a practice and buy a house also?" asked Janice.

"Yes, my grandfather, on my mother's side, set up trust funds for all of us. David used part of his to buy a house. He joined my dad in his car repair shop. He did not want to go to college, so he has a good bit of his trust fund left. Will is paying for his college out of his, but he will have plenty left. I won't have as much left, but I still have a sizable amount."

"I'm sorry," said Janice, "I'm being nosy. I guess it is the reporter in me. I'm used to asking questions."

"I don't mind." said Mike with a smile. "I want you to know all about me and my family. I also want to know all about you and your family."

"My parents passed away some years ago. All I have left is a sister. She is in college. I have been taking care of her for years, but she assures me she can take care of herself now," Janice smiled at Mike. "I guess I will just have to wait and see."

Their seafood salad had been left at their table and they had started eating it. They were so focused on each other that they hardly noticed what they were eating.

Janice glanced down at her plate then looked up at Mike in surprise. "This is really good," she said.

Mike smiled, "Yes, it is," he agreed.

After they finished their salad, they sat and talked while sipping their drinks. Finally, Mike realized it was getting late. He took the check, and adding a tip, gave the server his credit card to pay for it. As soon as she returned with his card and a receipt, he helped Janice from her chair and headed outside to his car. When he was beside his car, before he opened her door. He turned Janice toward him.

"I had a really nice time tonight," he whispered.

"Me, too," agreed Janice.

Mike pulled her close and kissed her. He ignored the shock at their touch and it soon went away.

"Ummm," said Janice as she snuggled closer.

Mike finally pulled back so they could catch their breath. He lay his forehead against Janice for a minute, then pulled back and opened her door for her. Janice climbed into the car. After fastening her seat belt, she rested her head against her head rest and sighed.

Mike heard the sigh when he entered the driver's seat. He smiled with satisfaction. They may have some problems to work out, but they had a strong attraction working for them.

Mike walked Janice to her motel room door and kissed her again before saying good night. After getting her phone number, he promised to call her the next morning. Janice floated into her room and sank down on the bed. She lay back and stared at the ceiling. She could hardly believe something so wonderful was happening to her.

Mike went home. He stopped on the porch and sat in the swing. He looked up at the stars and smiled. They would work through their problems. True love could not be denied.

The next morning, Janice called her sister.

"Hi, Sis, what's up? Why are you calling so early?" asked Brianna.

"Hi, I wanted to catch you before class," said Janice.

"Are you okay?" asked Brianna.

"I am better than okay. I'm in love," said Janice.

"Wow, he must be very special to get your attention," said Brianna.

"He is very special. The magic mirror showed him to me. I had a date with him last night. His kisses curl my toes," sighed Janice.

Brianna laughed. "I can't wait to meet him. Where does he live?"

"He lives in Denton. He is studying to be a veterinarian. He is almost ready to graduate. What do you think about moving to Denton when you graduate?" asked Janice.

"I would love to check it out. I would love to check out the magic mirror, too. Are you really thinking about moving there?" asked Brianna.

"Mike is here. He has parents and two brothers here. I only have an apartment and you. I can move everything in my apartment with no trouble. I spend very little time there anyway. I'm always on the road, chasing a story. You can come here as easily as there."

"What about your work?" Brianna asked.

"I'm doing mostly freelance now. I'm going to check out the local paper and see if they are interested in hiring me. If they aren't, I'll keep doing freelance. I can do it anywhere," said Janice.

"It sounds like you have made up your mind. I hope everything works out for you. When you decide to move let me know, so I can come and check out your new home and your toe-curling guy," said Brianna.

"I will. I love you. Keep in touch," said Janice.

"I love you, too," said Brianna.

Janice hung up the phone with a sigh of satisfaction. She was just about to get up when the phone rang.

"Hello," said Janice.

"Good morning, beautiful," said Mike.

Mike, good morning. I was just talking about you," said Janice.

"Oh, good things, I hope," said Mike.

"Very good, I was talking to my sister, Brianna. I told her about meeting you and the magic mirror. She is excited about meeting you and she wants to visit the magic mirror," said Janice.

Mike laughed. The magic mirror does draw a lot of attention," he said. "I am looking forward to meeting your sister. I am sure she will fit right in around here. My mom will love to have another girl around. She has been after us to give her some grandkids to fuss over. She is going to have a full house. She will love it."

"I am sure Brianna will love being fussed over, too. She has only had me for a long time. Having a large family around will be a new experience for her," said Janice.

"What are you doing today?" asked Mike.

"I am doing some more research on the magic mirror for my article," said Janice.

"I have a half day today. Do you want to meet when I get off?" asked Mike.

"Yes, give me a call and we can get together," said Janice.

"I can't wait to see you," said Mike.

"I can't wait to see you. I am looking forward to some more toe-curling," said Janice.

"What?" Mike asked.

"I told Brianna that your kisses were toe-curling," said Janice with a laugh.

Mike laughed. "I'll see what I can do."

"I'll be waiting," said Janice. She hung up the phone and smiled.

Mike hung up his phone smiling with satisfaction. "Toe-curling," he said with a laugh.

He went to get ready for work. The sooner he got to work, the sooner he could get away and see Janice again.

Janice went to shower and get breakfast. She wanted to swing by the local newspaper and check it out. She would have to get a move on if she was going to meet Mike for lunch.

CHAPTER 10

*J*anice had a very satisfactory visit with the editor of the local paper. He was very interested in having her work for his paper. She told him she would think about his offer and let him know in a few days.

When Mike finished work, he headed straight for Janice's motel. He called her to let her know he was on his way. When Janice opened her door, they both had smiles on their faces. Mike stepped inside, closed the door and pulled her into his arms. They both ignored the shock as he proceeded to kiss her. Janice put her arms around him and held him close as she kissed him back.

They were both breathless when they came up for air. After a brief pause, to catch their breath, they were kissing again. After he came up for air again, Mike smiled into Janice's eyes. "How is that for toe-curling?" he asked.

Janice laughed. "My toes will never be the same again," she said.

"I know what you mean. I think you did some toe-curling of your own," said Mike.

Janice laughed. "I talked to the editor of the local paper today. He offered me a job."

"I thought you were working freelance," said Mike.

"I am, but if I take a job with the paper here, I won't have to do as much traveling. I can still work freelance when I want to," she looked up into his eyes. She wanted to see if he was as committed to them being together as she was.

"If you take a job here, you will have to move here," said Mike. He started smiling again and pulled her closer. "I was going to talk to you about moving here, but I did not know how you would feel about moving. I even thought about looking into a veterinary practice where you are living now. I don't care where we live so long as we are together."

He proceeded to kiss her passionately. Janice kissed him back. Her doubts were all gone. He was as committed to her as she was to him. After several more very satisfying kisses, they proceeded to the sofa and sat down. Mike still had his arm around her, and she held tightly to his hand.

"I would never ask you to give up your family and your practice to move," said Janice.

"I want you to be happy. I don't want you to think you have to give up your life for us to be together," said Mike.

"I am not giving up anything," said Janice. "I have an apartment. I am hardly ever there. Brianna can come here as easily as there. I think she will like it better here. She will have family around to make her feel welcome. The main thing is we will be together. I have never felt this way before. I don't want to give up this toe-curling feeling."

Mike smiled. "Neither do I. I am not arguing against you moving here. I am all for it. We can start looking for a house. There is no need for you to stay in a motel. I'll talk to a realtor and see what is available. I'll also talk to Mom and Dad. They may know of some property the realtor does not have listed yet."

Mike looked down into her eyes and smiled. "How would you like to meet my mom and dad this evening? We need for them to meet you before we spring everything else on them." Janice looked serious.

"Mom is going to love you. So is Dad," he said reassuringly.

"I have never had to meet prospective parents before," said Janice.

"You are used to interviewing all types of people. You will be fine.

Just remember, they will be ready to love and accept you because I love you. You are ahead already, said Mike.

Janice squeezed his hand. "I know you are right. I am sure I will be fine after the meeting part is over."

Janice lay her head on his chest and sighed, Mike put his chin on top of her head and pulled her closer.

"I can't believe how fast everything has happened. I had no idea when I came looking for a story on the magic mirror it was going to change my life so completely. I still have to pinch myself to be sure I am not dreaming," Janice said.

"If it is a dream, we are going to be living in this dream world for a long time and I am going to be right by your side, loving you, through it all," declared Mike.

After another passionate kissing session, Mike rose and pulled Janice up with him. "We need to get something to eat and look around town a bit. I want you to see everything about your new hometown."

Janice smiled and allowed him to guide her to his car.

They stopped and picked up some burgers and fries. They ate while Mike drove around. He pointed out different shopping places around town. He showed her where David lived and pointed out the park across from David's house.

When they were driving around the park, they spotted a house for sale. It was on the opposite side of the park from David. Mike stopped in front of the house and studied the sign. It had the realtor number on it.

"What do you think?" he asked. "Would you like to look at the inside?"

"Yes," agreed Janice. "I love the large porch. Can't you just see us sitting out there in a swing, enjoying the sunset?"

Mike smiled and dialed the realtor. He talked for a minute, and then hung up.

"The realtor will be here in a few minutes," he said with satisfaction. Janice smiled and looked at the house. It was a dream come true. The realtor pulled into the driveway and went to unlock the house. Mike and Janice exited the car and went up to the porch.

"Hi," said Mike. "I'm Mike Murdoc. I'm the one who called you. This is Janice Slater."

"Hello," said the realtor offering her hand to shake. "I'm Dana Jenkins. You are lucky. This house was just listed this morning. The couple, who lived here, are moving out of state. He's in the army and she is expecting. He wanted her to be with her folks while he is gone. She is having a difficult pregnancy."

"We were just driving around and spotted the sign," said Mike.

They went inside to look around. They didn't talk much. The realtor pointed out a few things to them, but mostly Mike watched Janice to see what she was thinking about the place. It had a large spacious living area; the dining area was next. Janice smiled at the bar that led into the kitchen. The kitchen was fully equipped with all appliances.

"Do the appliances come with it?" asked Janice.

"Yes," replied Dana. "It also has the washer and dryer."

They then headed for the bedrooms. The master bedroom was large and spacious. It had an en- suite bathroom and a large walk-in closet.

"I like this," said Janice.

It had three more bedrooms and an office. Each of the bedrooms had spacious closets. There were two more bathrooms. One was in the hall and the other was between two of the bedrooms. They went back through the house and looked out of the back door. It had a large patio and a built-in grill. The large back yard had a fence around it.

"It has central air and heating," said Dana. "All of the utilities are on city lines."

Mike looked at Janice. She looked up at him and smiled.

"Do you like it?" he asked.

"Yes," she said.

"Okay," said Mike turning to Dana. "Let's go to your office and talk price."

Dana smiled. "Let me lock up and you can follow me to my office."

They waited in the car for Dana to lock up.

"Do you really think you can be happy here?" asked Mike.

"I can be happy anywhere you are," said Janice. "But I love the house."

Mike leaned over and kissed her.

In Dana's office at Jenkins Real Estate, she showed them the asking price and gave them a sheaf of papers to look over about the house.

While Mike looked over the papers, Janice smiled at Dana. "Is this your real estate firm?" asked Janice.

"It belongs to my husband and myself," answered Dana. "I was Bob's office manager before we were married. I don't usually handle showing houses. We have several agents. They were all out when you called. Since I took the listing this morning, I decided to show it to you."

Mike finished looking over the papers. "The price is very reasonable," he said.

"They were in a hurry to get everything settled before the husband ships out," agreed Dana.

"Okay," said Mike. "How long will it take to close on it?"

"It will depend on your financing," said Dana.

"I can have you a certified check for the full price here in the morning," said Mike.

Dana smiled. "The owners are still in town. I can get them in tomorrow to sign the sale papers. Then I will file all the paper- work and you will have a new home in a couple of days. You will be able to take the keys and have possession as soon as the signing is over."

"Okay, do you need any money to hold it?" asked Mike.

"No, since you are paying cash, I will make sure no one else shows it before tomorrow. Congratulations," said Dana standing and offering her hand. "You have a lovely new home. I hope you will be very happy in it."

"Thank you, I'm sure we will,' said Mike. Both he and Janice shook hands with Dana, and she walked them out.

When they were in the car, Janice looked at Mike.

"I must be dreaming," she said.

Mike smiled at her. "Why is that?" he asked

"You are making all of my dreams come true. If the magic mirror does this for others, I'm surprised it isn't being mobbed," said Janice.

"I don't know about others, but we are special," said Mike. "You ready to meet your future in-laws?" asked Mike.

"Yes," agreed Janice.

Mike squeezed her hand and held on to it as he headed to his parents' home. Lucy Murdoc was getting out of her car when Mike drove up and stopped. She stopped and waved at Mike. She looked in surprise at

Janice. Mike got out of his car and went around and helped Janice out of the car. They started walking toward Lucy. Mike had Janice's hand firmly in his.

"Mom, this is Janice Slater, the love of my life. Janice, meet Lucy Murdoc, the one who has put up with me all these years. Both Lucy and Janice laughed and shook hands.

"It's nice to meet you, Mrs. Murdoc," said Janice.

"It's nice to meet you, Janice," said Lucy.

"The magic mirror matched us, Mom," said Mike.

Lucy looked surprised. "I should have had Will go after the magic mirror ages ago," replied Lucy with a laugh.

"Why?" asked Mike, puzzled.

"Because ever since he tried to keep Alison from seeing in it, life seems to have sped up," said Lucy.

Mike pulled Janice close to his side as he reached the front door.

Lucy turned and opened the door for them. "Come on in, your dad should be here soon. David will be over as soon as he cleans up and picks up Bertha and Amos.

"I read your articles about the magic mirror, Janice." said Lucy.

"Will called me about doing another story on the mirror here," said Janice.

"I'm home," called Cam, from the front door. Lucy headed for the front door and gave Cam a kiss.

Janice watched and looked up at Mike with a smile. It would be wonderful to be a part of this loving family. Mike smiled down at her and kissed her on her nose.

Cam looked over Lucy's shoulder and spotted Janice. He smiled at Mike. "Our boys have great taste in ladies," he said to Lucy.

"Yes, come and meet Janice. Mike said the magic mirror matched them," said Lucy with a smile for Janice.

"The magic mirror has done this family proud," declared Cam, with a smile for Janice.

"Thank you," said Janice, as Cam came over and kissed her cheek.

"Welcome to the family, Janice," said Cam.

Lucy drew her into a hug. "Yes, you are a welcome addition to our family," she said.

"Did you say David and Bertha are coming over tonight?" asked Mike.

"Yes, they will be over in a little while. David was giving Bertha time to pick up Amos from daycare and get changed before picking them up," said Cam.

"I guess I need to get supper on the table," said Lucy.

"Can I help?" asked Janice.

"Sure," said Lucy. "I have it in the crock pot, but you can set the table. It will give us a chance to get better acquainted," said Lucy.

Janice gave Mike a smile and a hand-squeeze before following his mom into the kitchen.

Lucy showed Janice where to find dishes and silverware. She got the glasses ready for ice- tea. Lucy took some bread from the freezer and popped it in the oven. She had two chocolate cream pies. She set them on the counter to be cut later. Lucy took the ingredients for salad out and started washing and getting it ready to mix.

Janice came over and started tearing the lettuce into pieces for the salad. She took each vegetable, as Lucy cleaned it, and added it to the bowl of salad. While they were working, Janice told Lucy about her job offer with the local newspaper. She also mentioned Brianna. She told her about her parents' death and about taking care of Brianna.

Lucy listened and consoled her about her parents' death. She told her Brianna would be welcome in their home anytime. "I can't wait to meet her," declared Lucy. "If she's anything like her sister, I'm sure she is a lovely girl. This family has always needed some girls. Don't get me wrong. I love my boys. They are wonderful young men, but sometimes you just need some feminine company."

Janice laughed. "It sounds like you are going to have plenty of ladies around very soon," she said.

"Yes," agreed Lucy, happily.

Mike and his dad had the television on in the living room. They were talking quietly. The television was only providing background noise. They were not paying any attention to it. Mike was telling his dad about the house he had just purchased. "It's a great house," said Mike. "Janice loved it. I think we will be very happy there. And we will have plenty of room for Janice's sister, Brianna.

"I know the house you are talking about." said Cam. "You made a good choice."

"A good choice about what?" asked Lucy coming into the room with Janice following.

"Mike and Janice have bought a house across the park from David," said Cam.

"How did you find a house in that neighborhood?" asked Lucy. "There are hardly ever any houses for sale there."

"We were driving around and spotted the 'for sale' sign," said Mike. "We called the realtor and she came out and showed it to us. She said it had just been listed."

"Who was the realtor?" asked Cam.

"Dana Jenkins," replied Mike.

"Oh, she is Mallie's mom," said Lucy.

"Who's Mallie?" asked Mike.

"She's married to Daniel Grey from Grey's hardware store," said Lucy. "She and Daniel have a little girl of about four. Bertha's dad was telling me about them."

"Hello, is anyone here?" called David, opening the door and putting Amos down. Amos ran to give Lucy a hug. David came forward with his arm around Bertha. "I understand congratulations are in order," he said grinning at Mike and Janice.

Janice had stepped closer to Mike when David and Bertha had entered with Amos. Mike put his arm around and drew her to his side. "Janice, this is my brother David and his fiancée, Bertha. Guys this is the love of my life, Janice Slater."

"Hi, Janice welcome to the family," said David, leaning over and giving her a hug.

"Thank you," said Janice.

"Weren't you the one Will was trying to get to write a story about the magic mirror?" asked David.

"Yes," agreed Janice. "It was while I was checking the magic mirror out for the story, it showed me Mike."

"I saw David in the magic mirror, too," said Bertha.

Janice grinned at Bertha. "It was quite an experience," said Janice.

"Yes, it was. I was checking out the report of a break-in and the next thing I know, the magic mirror was showing me my true love," said Bertha with a smile.

"What is it with you guys and the magic mirror?" asked Janice looking around at the group.

Mike shrugged. "It likes us. Will is on its good side." Cam and Lucy joined in as everyone laughed at this comment.

"Come on everyone, let's eat," said Lucy. She hurried into the kitchen to take her homemade bread out of the oven.

Everyone else settled around the table and David put Amos in his booster chair. They all bowed their heads and gave thanks before starting to eat.

$\mathcal{W}$ill and Tim were working in the back room of the museum on Saturday when they heard a commotion in the room with the magic mirror. They hurried into the room to find two girls in each other's face, yelling at each other.

"What is going on here?" asked Will as he stepped between the girls.

"Lori claims she saw my boyfriend in the magic mirror," said one of the girls.

Will looked at Lori. He saw a satisfied smirk on her face.

"You claim to have seen this young lady's boyfriend in the magic mirror?" he asked.

"Yes," replied Lori.

"Did you see anyone in the mirror," asked Will of the other girl.

"My name is Shannon. I haven't looked in the magic mirror, yet."

"I see," said Will. "Do you want to look in it now?"

Shannon sat down and looked in the magic mirror. She shrugged and rose. "I didn't see anyone," she said.

"See," smirked Lori.

"Just because she didn't see her boyfriend in the mirror, doesn't mean you did," said Will. "Let's ask the magic mirror about it."

"How can the magic mirror tell us who was seen?" asked Shannon.

Lori looked startled. Will ignored the question as he sat down in front of the mirror. "I know you don't usually explain yourself, but I need your help," Will explained to the mirror. "Did Lori see anyone in your mirror?"

The magic mirror blinked once.

"I see," said Will. He looked at Lori and Shannon. "The magic mirror said Lori did see someone. Did she know the person she saw in the mirror?"

The mirror blinked.

"The magic mirror said yes," said Will. "Was the person Lori saw Shannon's boyfriend?"

The magic mirror blinked twice.

"The magic mirror said the person you saw was not Shannon's boyfriend," said Will.

Will rose and looked at Lori. "You do not tell lies about the magic mirror. When it shows you someone you have the choice of taking its advice or ignoring it, but don't misrepresent it. You don't want to chance its retaliation. Everyone has free will. You don't have to accept the magic mirror's showing. You can go on and ignore it completely and marry someone else. You may even make a comfortable life for yourself, but you will always feel an emptiness. It will be a feeling like something is missing. How you handle it is entirely up to you."

Will looked around at Tim and all the girls staring at him in amazement. He grinned at Shannon and took her hand.

"I don't know if your boyfriend is your true love or not. He may have not been close to a reflective surface when you looked in the magic mirror. The main thing is to trust your heart and don't let someone else tell you lies for spite. I hope everything works out for you," said Will.

"Thank you," said Shannon. She gave Lori a look and turned and left with her friends.

Lori looked at Will, "How did you know I wasn't telling the truth?" she asked.

"It was just a feeling," said Will. "The magic mirror confirmed it." Lori shrugged and turned and left.

Valerie came over to Will. "You handled the situation very well. Will," she said.

"Thank you," said Will.

Will and Tim turned and went back to work. "There's not a dull moment around you," said Tim, clapping Will on the back as they left.

"I have learned a lot since I met up with the magic mirror," said Will.

"How did you know Lori was not telling the truth?" asked Tim.

"It was something in her eyes. It was as if she was daring anyone to prove her wrong. I'm glad the mirror set us all straight. I never know how it is going respond. I just have to hope for the best," said Will as he resumed working.

Tim came over and started to help Will unpack and log in new merchandise for the museum.

"How are David and Officer Thorton getting along?" asked Tim.

"They are doing great," said Will. "You had better get used to calling her Bertha. She and David are engaged."

"Wow," exclaimed Tim. "Things sure happen fast in your family."

Will grinned. "Mike met his true love because of the mirror, too."

"Really," said Tim.

"Yep, and you will never guess who she is," said Will.

"Who?" Tim asked.

"Janice Slater," said Will.

Tim stopped and stared at Will. "You are not kidding me, are you?"

Will laughed. "They are all set to be together. She has even looked into getting a job locally."

"Wow," Tim shook his head. "When is my true love going to show up?"

"Be patient," said Will. "They are older than us. Our time is coming."

"I'll try," promised Tim.

They worked happily together for the rest of the day. There was a steady line of girls coming through the museum to look in the magic mirror. Word had spread about Lori and Shannon's confrontation and the magic mirror's response to it. The girls were more determined than ever to see if the magic mirror would show them their true love.

Mike and Janice had gone by and closed on their house. Mike had taken Janice by the jewelry store and purchased her an engagement ring. Now they were looking at furniture for their new house. They did not have to buy a lot. The former owners were leaving some furniture behind. They wanted new furniture in their bedroom, and they were making sure there was a room ready for Brianna.

Janice was keeping Brianna updated on everything. Brianna was very excited for her sister and was looking forward to meeting Mike and his family.

David, Bertha, Mike and Janice had sat down together and decided they were going to have a double wedding. They talked to Lucy and Cam about having the wedding in their back yard. Lucy and Cam thought it was a great idea. The wedding date was set for two months from then. They wanted to be sure Brianna and Will would be on break from classes and could attend without worrying about studying.

Mike had talked to Dr. Long and arranged to be away for a week after the wedding. David had found a budding mechanic to help Cam while he was away. He did not want Cam to have to manage by himself. The young lady was a senior high school student, but she was passionate about mechanic's work, and David was thinking about asking her to stay on after he and Bertha returned from their honeymoon.

Lucy, Bertha, and Janice were getting together and planning the wedding. Lucy was really enjoying herself, getting to know her future daughters-in-law. . Cam, Charlie, Mike and David were arranging for a tent to be put up in the back yard. Charlie was in charge of making sure they had chairs for the ceremony. He also arranged for tables to be set up for food.

The ladies, from Lucy's church group, had volunteered to help supply food for the reception. Bertha and Janice were skeptical about them helping. They suggested getting a caterer, but Lucy did not want to hurt anyone's feelings, so they agreed with the ladies helping.

Bertha's partner, Doug Perkins, had a sister who owned a flower shop. She agreed to talk to Doug's sister about the flowers. Bertha was sure she could get a good price on the flowers.

The ladies were meeting in the dining room at Cam and Lucy's'.

The guys had gotten together at the repair shop.

"We had better wrap this up for now," said Lucy taking their lists and putting them aside. "The guys will be coming in soon wanting something to eat."

"Yeah, I need to go and pick Amos up from daycare," said Bertha. "I came here straight from work and Dad was meeting the guys at the repair shop."

"I'll help Mom get food ready," said Janice. Lucy turned and looked at Janice. She looked like she was about to cry, "You don't mind me calling you mom, do you?"

Lucy went over and gave her a hug. "I love it, I don't mind at all. I hope you both will call me mom," she said tearfully.

Bertha joined in the hug. "I would love to call you mom. I haven't had a mom in a long time," she said.

After a little more hugging and wet eyes, Bertha left to go pick up Amos. Lucy and Janice went to look in the refrigerator to see what they could fix for supper. When they had food cooking, Lucy called Will.

"Hi, Mom," said Will.

"Are you through for the day?" asked Lucy.

"Yes, Tim and I are just leaving the museum," said Will.

"Good, we are all getting together at home for supper. You and Tim can join us. You need to get better acquainted with your future sisters-in-law," said Lucy.

"Mom wants us to come and eat," Will said to Tim.

"Sure," agreed Tim.

"We will be there, Mom. We have to go by the dorm and shower then we will be right over," said Will.

"Okay," said Lucy we will see you then." Lucy hung up her phone and turned to Janice and smiled. "We are going to have a house full," she said with satisfaction.

Janice laughed. She could see how happy it made Lucy to be surrounded by her family.

"Let's put another extension in the table so we will all fit," suggested Lucy. She headed to the pantry to get the extension.

Janice helped her to extend the table. After cleaning the table off, Janice took down the dishes and silverware and started setting the table. They decided to put the food on the counter and let everyone fill their plates there so they would have more room at the table. They were putting the food out when Bertha came in with Amos. Amos wiggled to get down and ran to give Lucy a hug.

"Here's my boy," exclaimed Lucy happily. Amos hugged her tightly. "Do you want to bring some toys in here to play with?" she asked Amos.

Amos nodded his head. He had a big smile on his face as Lucy took his hand to take him to get some toys to play with.

Bertha shook her head and smiled at Janice. "Amos is so happy to have more grandparents," she said.

"They make wonderful grandparents," said Janice.

"Our kids are going to be very lucky," agreed Bertha.

Everyone started arriving. David headed for Bertha and drawing her into his arms, kissed her soundly. Amos ran to David and was hugged. Mike drew Janice into his arms and kissed her, also. Cam came over and kissed Lucy. Charlie looked on and watched the happy group. He was glad to be a part of them.

They had turned toward the dining room when Will and Tim joined them. After they had greeted everyone, they entered the dining room. There was a knock at the door, and everyone stopped again. Mike grinned at Janice. "I think your surprise is here," he said, looking at Janice.

"My surprise?" she asked, smiling at him.

Mike opened the door and stood to the side so that Janice could see who was there.

"Brianna!" exclaimed Janice, as she hurried forward to hug her sister.

"Hi," said Brianna, hugging her back.

"What are you doing here? What about class?" asked Janice.

"We have a few days off, so when Mike asked me to visit and sent me a plane ticket, I came right away."

"I am so glad you did." Janice turned her around to face everyone. "Everyone, this is my sister Brianna. Brianna, this handsome guy beside me is Mike."

"Hello, Brianna," said Mike giving her a hug.

"Hi," said Brianna.

"This is Cam and Lucy, my new mom and dad," said Janice coming to a stop in front of Cam and Lucy.

Lucy stepped forward and gave Brianna a hug and Cam kissed her cheek. "Welcome to the family, Brianna," said Lucy.

"Thank you," said Brianna. She was a little overwhelmed with all the attention.

Janice pointed to David and Bertha. "This is David. He is Mike's brother. The lady beside him is Bertha, his fiancée. The little boy is Amos."

Brianna smiled at everyone and said hello. She looked over at Will and Tim. Janice saw where her attention was. "This is Mike's younger brother, Will and his friend Tim," said Janice.

Brianna absently smiled at Will and said hello. She was staring at Tim. Tim was staring back at her. He hadn't taken his eyes off her since she had arrived.

Brianna smiled at Tim. It was like he was being pulled by a string as he made his way toward her. He stopped in front of her and smiled into her eyes. He reached for her hand, but when they touched, they both jerked back their hands at the shock. He reached for her hand again and held on. The shock eased as they held hands.

"Will you marry me?" asked Tim earnestly.

"Yes, when I get out of college," replied Brianna.

"Okay," said Tim. "I have to finish, too."

Everyone looked on in amazement at the scene taking place in front of them. "I don't need the magic mirror to tell me we are meant to be together," said Tim.

"Me neither," agreed Brianna.

"Alright everyone," said Lucy. "Let's eat."

They all headed for the dining room. Brianna and Tim were still holding hands.

Will shook his head as he followed Tim and Brianna. There was never a dull moment in the Murdoc family, he thought with a smile.

David helped Amos into his seat while Bertha fixed him a plate. Everyone else grabbed their plates and headed for the counter to fill them.

Will moved the chairs around so Tim and Brianna could sit next to each other. Tim had finally let go of her hand so she could fill her plate, but he stayed close to her. Brianna did not object. She seemed to want to be close to him, too.

Janice shook her head as she gazed at her sister. She couldn't believe how fast everything had happened. At least the two of them realized they needed to finish college. She looked at Mike and sighed. She couldn't say anything. It had happened just as fast for her and Mike. Mike looked at her and grinned. He reached over and squeezed her hand.

"Tim's a good guy," he said. "I've known him all of his life. He has spent as much time in our house as in his."

"I know," agreed Janice. "It is just hard for me to see how grown up my little sister is."

"It will be alright. They still have a couple of years of college left," said Mike. Janice smiled and squeezed his hand.

"This food is great, Mom," said Janice.

Lucy beamed at her. "Thank you," she said. David, Mike and Will all smiled to see their mom so happy. Cam looked around the table and smiled at Charlie. Charlie smiled back. They were indeed blessed.

CHAPTER 12

Tim asked for Brianna's phone number when he saw Janice and Mike were getting ready to leave. He and Brianna had not had much of a chance to talk. They mostly just stayed close to each other and held hands.

Brianna handed Tim her phone and he entered his number in it and then he called his number. When his phone rang, he saved Brianna's number to his phone.

The two of them followed everyone out onto the porch as they were all saying goodnight to Mike and Janice. David and Bertha were getting Amos ready to go, also. Charlie had already said good night and headed home.

"I'll see you tomorrow at church," said Tim softly to Brianna.

"Yes," agreed Brianna.

"I have to work at the museum after church, but we can go out to eat after I get off work," said Tim.

"I would like to spend some time alone with you," agreed Brianna.

Tim leaned forward and kissed her gently. Brianna smiled at him and went to join Mike and Janice in Mike's car. She got into the back seat and, after putting on her seat belt; she leaned her head back and smiled dreamily.

Janice glanced back at Brianna. She shook her head. She knew the look. She had been seeing it on her own face for several days. Janice glanced over at Mike and smiled. He was concentrating on his driving and did not see her smile. Janice looked around when Mike stopped in the drive of their new house.

"Are we going to show Brianna the house tonight?" asked Janice.

Mike smiled. "I had the furniture store deliver and set up the bedrooms for us today. I also had groceries delivered. Everything should be set for you and Brianna to stay here tonight," said Mike.

"Oh my," said Janice hurrying out of the car and heading for the house.

Mike helped Brianna out and smiled as they followed Janice to the front door. Janice was waiting for them just inside the door.

Brianna looked around, wide-eyed, as they entered. "I love it," said Brianna.

"Wait until you see your room," said Janice. "Of course, you will want to put your own personal touch on it, but we are off to a good start." She took Brianna's arm and led her to her room.

"It's beautiful," said Brianna. She walked around, touching the dresser, the spread on the bed, and running her hand over table beside the bed.

"We'll let you get settled in and then I will show you the rest of the house," said Janice as Mike brought in Brianna's bag, Janice gave Brianna one last hug and followed Mike to the front room.

"Thank you," said Janice. She hugged him close and reached for a kiss.

"I want you both to be happy," said Mike. "I love you and when you are happy, I am happy."

He kissed Janice again and held her close. "I have to get started on another story about the magic mirror. I am so happy, I want to give others a chance to be happy, also," said Janice between kisses.

Mike laughed. "I am going to work on my kisses if you are still thinking about the mirror while I am kissing you," said Mike.

Janice kissed him again. "There's nothing wrong with your kisses. They still curl my toes."

Mike kissed her one more time and then pulled back. "I had better go and let you catch up with your sister. If you have any problems, call me. I'll see you in the morning."

He reluctantly said good night and left. Janice locked the door behind him and went in search of Brianna.

Brianna was finishing up putting her things away. She had not brought a lot with her. She turned and smiled at Janice. "I love my room. Thank you and Mike for making it so nice for me," she said.

Janice crossed to her and hugged her. "Of course, we made it nice for you. You are my sister. I want you to be happy here."

Brianna sat on the side of the bed and looked at Janice.

"What do you think about me switching to the college here to finish my studies?" asked Brianna.

Janice sat down beside her. "I don't know. Will you be able to transfer all of your grades?" asked Janice.

"I don't know. I will have to check on it. I wanted to be sure you were okay with me staying here with you while finishing my classes at the college here," said Brianna.

Janice put her arm around Brianna. "Is this about Tim?"

"Partly," agreed Brianna. "It's also about you and Mike. We haven't had a real home in a long time. I want to enjoy it. I also love feeling like I am part of a big family."

Janice hugged her. "We'll check it out on Monday. If it's possible, I would love having my sister close," said Janice. They hugged once more, both were teary-eyed.

"You get some rest. I'm going to take a shower and get ready to turn in. See you in the morning,"

"Good night," responded Brianna as Janice left.

Brianna was getting ready to lie down when her phone rang. She answered it quickly before it disturbed Janice.

"Hello," said Brianna.

"Hi," said Tim. "I wanted to say good night one more time. I have just seen you and I miss you already."

"I know." said Brianna. "I will be glad when tomorrow comes. I asked my sister about transferring to college here."

"What did she say?" asked Tim.

"She said we would check on it Monday," said Brianna.

"I'll keep my fingers crossed for us," responded Tim. Brianna laughed softly. "What are you taking in college?" asked Tim.

"I'm studying to be a teacher. I have a major in math and a minor in science."

"I'm studying to be a teacher, too. My major is history and my minor is Math," said Tim.

"Wow," said Brianna. "We have more in common than feelings."

"Yeah," agreed Tim. "We are made for each other. The moment I looked into your face, I knew you and I were meant for each other."

"I know. I felt it to," agreed Brianna.

"I hate to hang up, but we both need our sleep. I love you," said Tim.

"I love you, too," said Brianna. "I'll see you tomorrow." They hung up their phones and both lay on their backs, looking at the ceilings in their rooms. They lay, dreaming, until drifting off to sleep.

The next morning, Tim and Will waited in front of the church for Brianna, Janice and Mike to arrive. As soon as Mike parked his car, Tim hurried over to open Brianna's door and help her out of the car. He held her hand as they followed Mike, Janice and Will into the church. They sat on the same pew, with Mike and Janice going first and then Will. Tim let Brianna sit next and then he sat next to her.

Alison and Beth were seated in a pew closer to the front. When Alison looked back and saw a lovely new girl seated beside Will, she was startled. She stared at her for a minute, then turned and faced toward the front. She leaned closer to Beth.

"Do you know who the girl sitting beside Will is?" she asked.

Beth glanced over her shoulder and quickly looked forward again when a church lady sitting behind her gave her a stern look.

"I don't know. I have never seen her before," said Beth, softly.

The pastor came in and the service began. Alison and Beth were very distracted during the service. When it was over, they hurried to try and find out more about the new girl. They were delayed by the other church-goers and when they managed to get outside, Will and Tim had left for the museum and work. Mike and Janice had taken Brianna to show her around town. They insisted she needed to know more about the town before she decided to move there.

"We would love to have you move here," said Mike. "We want to make sure you will be happy with us."

"I will love being close to you and Janice," said Brianna. "Besides, Tim is here. We may not be planning to get married until we finish college, but I don't want to be so far away from him."

"I know how you feel," said Janice, squeezing Mike's hand and looking at him with love.

"Yes, so do, I," agreed Mike. "We will help any way we can."

Valerie was waiting for Will and Tim when they entered the museum. "I want you to dismantle this display." Valerie pointed at a display that had been in the front a long time. "Pack it carefully and put it in the storeroom. Then, I want you to go through the new things you have been checking in and design a new display to take its place. I will leave it up to you to pick which articles to display," said Valerie. "I think it will be less confusing for our patrons if the display is changed while the museum is closed."

"Sure," said Will with a smile. "This will be fun. I have been wondering when some of the new things were going to be used."

"Well," said Valerie with a smile, "I'll let you get to it. I have a date with my husband." With another smile and a wave, she left and locked the door as she went out. Valerie had given Will a key to the back door after he had been working there for a couple of weeks.

Will and Tim went about taking down the old display. Tim got some boxes from the back to pack it in and they carefully stored it in the storage room. After putting away the old display, they went to look over the new merchandise to see what they could put in its place. They found some statues of civil war soldiers. They carried three of them to the front. They placed one standing straight and tall, holding the American flag. One was kneeling and holding a southern flag. The other was standing back from the other two and was saluting the two flags. Will and Tim stood back and looked at the display.

"What do you think?" asked Will.

"I think she will love it or hate it. There is no, in between," said Tim.

Will looked at it and frowned. "Do you think we should change it?" he asked.

"No, absolutely not," said Tim. "If she doesn't like it, we can change it later, but we need to wait and see what she says first."

"Okay," said Will. "I know you have a date and we are finished here." They left through the back door. Will locked up after they went out.

"If you drop me of at the dorm, you can use my car," said Will.

"Thanks," said Tim.

He hurriedly dropped Will off and called Brianna to see if she was ready to be picked up.

Brianna gave him the address of Mike and Janice' house and said she would be waiting.

Brianna was waiting on the porch when Tim stopped out front. She started to go down to meet him, but Tim quickly left the car and joined her on the porch. He took her hand as soon as he stepped close to her. They ignored the tingle and held on.

"Hi," said Tim.

"Hi," said Brianna.

They stood holding hands and looking in each other's eyes.

Janice and Mike, watching from inside, looked on in amusement. "Should we go out and say something," asked Janice.

"No, let them work it out. I know how they feel. I feel the same way when I gaze into your eyes. I don't want to take away a moment of the wonder from them," said Mike.

Janice snuggled close in his arms.

"You may be right. It does feel wonderful. This magic should be savored," declared Janice. She raised her face for a kiss. Mike was happy to oblige her.

Tim and Brianna finally tore their eyes apart long enough to get into the car and drive to a restaurant. Once there, they ordered and sat gazing into each other's eyes while they nibbled on their food. Afterwards, neither, Brianna nor Tim could tell you what they had eaten, but they were very satisfied with their date. Both declared they had a wonderful time.

When Tim delivered Brianna back at the house, Tim kissed her goodnight and floated back to Will's car. He drove to the dorm and went inside. When Will asked him if he had a good time, Tim stared at him for a minute before answering. It was like he was coming out of a trance.

"Oh, yes," said Tim with a big smile. "I had a wonderful time."

Brianna did not even notice Mike and Janice seated on the sofa in the living room. She went past them and up the stairs to her room in a daze. She sat down at her dresser and started brushing her hair. Brushing her hair always calmed her and helped her to think. After a few minutes, she lay the brush down and smiled into the mirror.

"He's mine," she said to the mirror with satisfaction. She rose and went to prepare for bed.

CHAPTER 13

$\mathcal{V}$ alerie looked in amazement at the display arranged by Will and Tim. Will and Tim were not there. They were in class. Valerie started smiling. Her confidence in Will had not been misplaced. He had done a great job. His fresh look would draw more people into the museum, even if it were to protest. She couldn't wait to have the guys work out some of the older displays and set up new ones.

Will hurried over to the museum after he finished his classes for the day. Tim did not go with him. He had plans with Brianna. Valerie was in the front room when he entered. She gave him a big smile.

"Do you like it?" asked Will.

"I think it is great," responded Valerie. "I just have one question. Why do you have the one with the rebel flag kneeling?"

"Well, the South lost the war. I was trying to show that even though the South lost, both flags deserved respect and should be treated with respect.

"I think we should put up a sign by the display with those very words on it," said Valerie. "Could you write down what you said, and I will get the sign shop print it on a board for me."

"Sure, I can write it down for you now," said Will taking out a piece of paper and writing down what he had said. He handed the paper to Valerie.

"Thanks," said Valerie. "While you are here, I like your display so much I am going to have you switch some of the other ones. We will go slowly at first, maybe one every few days. We want to keep people coming back to see what we are up to."

Will laughed. "We can keep them guessing," he replied.

"Exactly," agreed Valerie with a smile.

"Just let me know which ones you are ready to put into storage and I'll see what I can come up with," promised Will.

Valerie took him around and pointed out three displays she wanted to put into storage. Will took note of them and then left to go back to the dorm and do his homework. Valerie closed early. She had a special evening planned with her husband. Valerie stopped by Marshal's restaurant and picked up an order she had called in earlier. She did not want to cook, and she did not want to spend the evening in a crowded restaurant.

Valerie took the food and set it on the counter at home. She went to her bedroom, took a shower and put on a sexy dress. She then went out into the dining room and set the table with their best dishes and put a nice flower arrangement with candles in the center of the table.

"Hello," said Marcus coming up behind her and drawing her into his arms from behind.

Valerie turned in his arms to face him and raised her face for a kiss.

"Hello," she said. "I didn't hear you come in."

Marcus kissed her again. "Are we expecting company?" he asked, looking at the table she had set and the food she was putting out.

"No," said Valerie with a smile. "I wanted you all to myself and I did not feel like going out. By the way, if Aunt Emily asks you, you had to work late today."

"Okay," agreed Marcus with a laugh. "You had better answer the phone or she will know something is up."

Valerie answered the ringing phone. "Hello, Aunt Emily, yes as a matter of fact Marcus managed to get away sooner than expected, but he doesn't feel like going anywhere. He's going to take a shower and relax a while. We will talk to you tomorrow, Aunt Emily."

Valerie hung up the phone to find Marcus laughing.

"She saw your car turn into our drive as she was on her way home," explained Valerie.

"What's up?" asked Marcus. "You usually don't mind Mom visiting."

"I love Aunt Emily, but tonight is for us," said Valerie snuggling close and kissing her husband. "Now, go take your shower while I put the food on the table."

"Yes, Ma'am," said Marcus, kissing her one last time before leaving.

Valerie finished arranging the food in bowls and put them out on the table. Marcus came back just as she had finished putting glasses of iced tea on the table. After he held her chair, they sat down to eat.

When they had finished eating, they both carried the dishes to the kitchen and Valerie loaded the dishwasher while Marcus put away the leftovers.

Valerie took Marcus' hand and led him to the living room. She looked up into his face and smiled. "I have a surprise," she said.

Marcus looked in her face. It was shining with excitement.

"We are going to be parents. I'm expecting."

Marcus looked at her for a moment, then, he drew her close and kissed her passionately. When he pulled back, he looked as excited as Valerie. They settled onto the sofa with his arms around her and talked about the coming baby. In between kisses they talked about names.

"You know we need to let Mom know. She will be so excited to know she is going to be a grandmother," said Marcus.

"I'll let her know tomorrow. Tonight, is just for us," said Valerie. "I'll have to call my folks, also. They will be so happy. They will probably pay us a visit."

"Okay," agreed Marcus.

They settled more comfortably on the sofa and held each other close.

"I have been thinking," said Valerie.

"What about?" asked Marcus between kisses on her neck.

"I think I would like to cut back on my time at the museum when I get further along in the pregnancy. After the baby comes, I may stay at home and be an at home mom," Valerie looked at Marcus to see how he was taking her words.

Marcus paused in his kissing and smiled. "You know whether you work or not is entirely up to you. I just want you to be happy."

"I was thinking, Will would do a good job of being a curator at the museum. I could stay on in an advisory capacity as long as he needed me. I'm pretty sure I could get Mr. Ames to agree. I checked with a friend at the college. She said Will has excellent grades and is well liked. He is majoring in business and has a minor in art appreciation. I think he would do very well at the museum. I have not said anything to him about it. I thought I would let him finish up his agreed time for breaking into the museum first." Valerie paused and looked at Marcus. "What do you think?" she asked.'

"I think you have some time before anything has to be decided. You can keep an eye on Will and see how everything goes. In a few months you will have a better feel for how he is doing. Nothing has to be decided in a hurry."

"I know you are right," said Valerie with a sigh. "I am just so excited about the baby that my mind is working overtime."

"I think I can help keep your mind occupied," said Marcus. He scooped her up into his arms and headed for their bedroom, kissing her all the way.

"Hmmmm," said Valerie when he paused. "More."

He was happy to oblige.

The wedding plans were coming together nicely. With the wedding getting closer, Bertha knocked on her captain's door. She wanted to be sure of getting two weeks off. She needed time before the wedding to get ready and David was planning for a week on the beach in Florida for a honeymoon.

Bertha knocked on the captain's door and waited for an answer.

"Come in," called the captain. "What can I do for you Officer Thorton?" he asked, seeing Bertha at the door.

"Sir, I want to put in for two weeks' vacation time," said Bertha.

The captain looked at Bertha closely before answering.

"I understand congratulations are in order," said the captain.

"Yes, sir," said Bertha. "I'm marrying David Murdoc."

"The Murdocs are fine people. I know you went through a rough time after the death of Officer Hayes. I'm glad you and your son are going on with your lives."

"Thank you, sir," responded Bertha.

"You may take all the time off you need. Turn in your request to the clerk and I will approve it." He came around his desk and held out his hand for a hand- shake. "I wish you and Mr. Murdoc the best in the future." Bertha shook his hand, said thank you and hurried out to hand her request to the clerk.

David had been making his own arrangements. He talked to a couple of their part time helpers to see if they would work full time while he was gone. He didn't want his dad working by himself while he was gone. Both helpers seemed happy to get the extra work and agreed immediately to cover for him. He was going to check on them when he returned to see if they needed help.

Janice was not due to start working at the local newspaper until after her honeymoon. She was determined to get the article on the magic mirror done and turned in before the wedding.

Mike had talked to Dr. Long about taking time off. Even though Dr. Long had been cutting back on the time he spent in the clinic, he was willing to come in full time while Mike was on his honeymoon. Everything was working out fine. They were almost ready for the wedding to take place.

Brianna had gone to the college office and inquired about transferring to the college in Denton. She explained that her sister was marrying Mike Murdoc and would be living in Denton. She told them she wanted to be closer to her family as a reason for transferring. They were checking on everything to see if her scholarship and all of her grades could be transferred. They were hopeful everything would be okay.

Everyone met back at the Murdoc family home and reported in about all of their plans being ready for a go ahead. Brianna told them about seeking a transfer to the college in Denton.

Lucy waited until they were all occupied doing other things and slipped into her bedroom and closed her door. She took her cell phone with her. She called her friend Pam, who worked in the office at the college.

"Hello, Pam, this is Lucy Murdoc. How are you doing? "

"I am doing okay. How about you?" Pam asked.

"I am fine. I am calling about a student, Brianna Slater. She is wanting to transfer to Denton College," said Lucy"

"Yes, I talked to Miss Slater today. I see no trouble with the transfer if we can get her scholarship to transfer with her. She said she did not have the funds to transfer without the scholarship."

"I want you to approve her transfer. If her scholarship doesn't transfer, I will set up a scholarship for her. I don't want anyone to know about me setting up this scholarship. It is a one-time deal," said Lucy.

"Okay, Lucy, I will let you know as soon as I have any information," agreed Pam.

"Thank you, Pam," said Lucy and hung up. Lucy smiled with satisfaction. She did not use the trust fund her father had arranged for her very often, but she wanted to make sure all of her new family got off to the best start possible.

Lucy did not say anything to the family about calling the college when she rejoined them. They were all in a happy mood, talking and laughing, Later, when she and Cam retired for the night, she told Cam what she had done.

"I am proud of you," he said holding her close and kissing her. "I would say you put your dad's money to good use."

"I know," said Lucy. "I want Brianna to be happy here. I know she would not be happy if she could not stay close to Tim. I am so glad those two found each other."

"They make a fine couple," agreed Cam.

"How long do you think it will be before we can expect grandkids?" Lucy asked.

Cam chuckled. "I think we have to leave the grandkids up to fate. You will have to be satisfied with Amos for the time being."

"I love Amos," said Lucy. "I just want to hold a little baby in my arms again."

Cam smiled as he held Lucy close and kissed her. "Have I told you lately how much I love you?"

"I always love hearing it again. I love you, too,' she said, as she kissed him back.

The two of them did not talk any more for a while.

～

Will told Tim how much Valerie had liked the display. He explained about the additional displays she wanted them to arrange.

"Cool," said Tim. "It will be nice to cause a stir in town without getting into trouble."

Will laughed. "Everyone is so busy at home. They are getting ready for the weddings. Working will give me an excuse to stay out of the way. If I didn't have to work, Mom would keep me busy running errands."

"I wouldn't mind running errands," said Tim. "I might be able to get Brianna to run errands with me."

"Just drop by the house. I'm sure Mom will put you to work," said Will.

"I just might do that," said Tim. He took his phone and called Brianna to wish her a goodnight.

Will went to take a shower to give Tim and Brianna a little privacy. Tim and Brianna were still talking when Will came out of the shower. Will sat down to study and put his earphones in his ears. He turned some music on low so he could listen to it while he did his homework.

Tim hung up his phone and smiled when he saw Will with his earphones in his ears. He was shaking his head slightly to the sound of music while doing his work. Tim pulled out his books and started doing his homework.

Will was thinking about Alison. They had not been out together since his accident. They saw each other in class and at church. Although they were always friendly, something was missing. The old excitement was no longer there. He liked her and wanted the best for her, but just didn't think he was the right one for her He would just have to wait and see who the magic mirror sent his way. He had plenty of time. There was no rush. The work at the museum was exciting and fulfilling for him. When he finished college, it was just the type of work he wanted to do.

Will and Tim finished their work and turned in for the night; Tim with a smile on his face as he thought of Brianna and Will with a calmness that came with knowing which direction he wanted to go with his future.

CHAPTER 14

The Magic Mirrors – By Janice Slater

The magic mirrors do exist. There are three of them. The silver mirror is in The Gallery in Rolling Fork. The copper one is in The Museum in Denton. The gold one is in Danny's Bar and Grill in Sharpville. They were purchased in Italy by the owners of The Gallery. The Gallery owners wanted as many girls as possible to look in the mirrors, so they sent them to different locations. If a girl, or woman, looks in the mirror it will sometimes show them their true love. They really work. I was amazed when I looked in the mirror in Denton and saw my true love looking back at me. His smiling face will be in my heart forever.
I have recently learned the mirror does more than show true love. When a young man tried to keep his girlfriend from looking in the mirror in Denton, he accidentally dropped and broke the mirror. Lightning-like streams of light shot out and hit the face of the young man. He had blisters and his eyesight was blurred. The broken mirror, somehow, put itself back together and the young man was taken to the hospital. After being told by the doctors it would take time to heal, the young man was sent home.

The young man did not go straight home. He went by the museum and apologized to the magic mirror for interfering with its job. The magic mirror accepted his apology and a soft white light came from the mirror and enveloped the young man. When the light went away, the young man's face was healed, and his eyesight was clear. Even though the magic mirror retaliates when threatened, it shows mercy when it senses sincere regret for an action.

Many girls and young women have met their true loves through the magic mirror, and I hope many more are lucky enough to see their true loves gazing back at them. So, if you want to try and see your true love ladies, make a stop at one of the three magic mirrors and have a look. Will you be one of the lucky ones to find true love? You will not know until you try. Good luck and best wishes.

*J*anice wrapped up her article and smiled with satisfaction. She sent a copy to the local newspaper and made sure another copy went to the wire services, she wanted the article to have as wide a coverage as possible.

Pam, from the office at the college, called Lucy the next day. Brianna's grades could all be transferred, but part of her financial aid could not be transferred. Lucy assured Pam the aide would be in place by the next day. When Lucy hung up her phone, after talking to Pam, she called her attorney who was handling her trust fund. She instructed him to set up a fifty-thousand-dollar scholarship program for the Murdoc family at the college. She told him to make Brianna the first recipient. The college was not to use any of the funds without approval from the Murdoc family. She instructed him to make funds available for Brianna at once.

While she was talking to him, she asked him to set up another trust fund for Amos Thorton in the amount of fifty thousand dollars. He was not to have access to it until he turned twenty-five. The attorney assured her he would have both funds set up and would have someone bring papers over for her to sign later in the day.

When Lucy hung up, she was well satisfied with her actions. She called Cam at the shop and told him what she had done.

Cam smiled as he listened. "I'm glad you could help," he said. "I have been meaning to talk to you about Amos. We have had so much going on I kept forgetting. I'm glad you can read my mind." Cam laughed. "I love you."

"I love you, too. You must have been projecting really loudly," said Lucy, with a laugh.

"No," said Cam. "We are so close we can almost be one mind. I am so glad I have you in my life."

"I am glad we have each other," said Lucy.

"I'll see you in a little while," said Cam, as he hung up.

When he hung up the phone, he turned to find David grinning at him from the door.

Cam looked at him sternly, "What are you grinning about?"

"I was just hoping Bertha and I have as much love between us in thirty years as you and Mom. It is great to see you so happy," said David.

"Love takes work," said Cam. "You have to love and respect your partner. You have to remember you are partners and she has an equal say. No one is boss. Listen to her when she talks and respect her opinions. When you have love to cushion your actions, it makes it easier. If you mess up, admit it. Do your best to make things right." David started to speak, but Cam held up his hand, "You will mess up. We all do. Just don't waste any time making things right when you do. Love is a wonderful thing, but like I said, it takes work."

"Thanks, Dad," said David, coming over and standing by Cam. "I will remember what you said."

David turned and went back into the shop. Cam sat staring into space for a minute before getting up and following.

Later that evening, David and Bertha were snuggling on the sofa at his house. They had been getting the house ready for them all to live in. Amos' room had been decorated to suit a small boy. He even had a child sized bed, shaped like a car. Amos was in awe of it.

He decided to take a nap in his car before going home for the night.

"I've been thinking," said David softly as he kissed Bertha's neck.

"What about?" asked Bertha.

"If it's okay with you, I want to adopt Amos. I want him to have the Murdoc name and to always know he is my son and the older brother to any other kids we have."

Bertha kissed him and smiled. "I think it's a wonderful idea. Amos already thinks of you as his dad. I know he will like having the same last name after we are married."

"I'll talk to my lawyer tomorrow and get him started on the adoption," said David in between kisses.

"I need to gather up Amos and go home so I can get some sleep," said Bertha.

"You don't have to work tomorrow. Why don't you stay here? Let Amos enjoy his new bed. It is just a few more days until the wedding. If you don't want to share my bed, you can take the extra room beside Amos."

"Who said I didn't want to share your bed?" asked Bertha. She leaned back and looked at David and smiled.

"Are you sure?" asked David. "I don't want to rush you."

"I'm sure. Rush me," said Bertha, drawing him in close for another kiss.

David kissed her passionately. He took her in his arms, and stumbled toward his room, kissing all the way. He almost bumped into the door he was so distracted.

Bertha laughed at him when he dodged the door. She soon quit laughing and joined once more in the love-making.

The next morning, Janice's article came out. Everyone was talking about it. There was a flood of girls in the museum, wanting to see the magic mirror for themselves. Valerie called Will and asked him if he could come over after class. He agreed.

He decided to take Tim along with him. When he arrived at the museum, he could barely squeeze in. He looked around in amazement. He had never imagined the museum being this crowded. He and Tim waved at Valerie and worked their way into the room with the magic mirror. The girls were shoving each other trying to get to the mirror. Some of the girls were standing back, shaking their heads. They looked like they were about to change their minds about staying.

Will pushed his way to the mirror and stood between the group and the mirror. "If you want to look in the magic mirror," said Will. "You are going to do so in an orderly way with no pushing and shoving. The magic mirror does not like being disrespected."

The girls stopped arguing and stared at Will. He motioned for the first girl to sit in front of the mirror. She sat down and gazed into the mirror. Nothing happened. She gave a sigh of disappointment and rose to leave. The next girl sat down and looked in the mirror. She was disappointed also.

It went on. The girls sat down, one at a time, and looked in the mirror. No-one was seeing anyone. Will turned aside and spoke to Tim softly. "Do you think the magic mirror is upset because of all the fuss the girls made?" he asked.

"I don't know," said Tim with a shrug. "I suppose it is possible."

Will waited for some more of the girls to look in the mirror. He finally stopped them from looking anymore. "Girls, I don't think the magic mirror is going to show anything now. I think it is upset by all of the arguing. You are welcome to look, but I think it would be better if you came back some other time."

Some of the girls started leaving. They were disappointed but they listened to what he said and agreed.

After most of the girls were gone, two girls stayed behind. They came over to Will beside the magic mirror. "Hi, my name is Lacy, and my friend's name is Marion. We came over from the next county to look in the magic mirror and we can't come back tomorrow. Would it be alright if we looked in the magic mirror? It's very important,' said Lacy.

Will smiled. "Sure, I don't know if it is going to do any good, but you are welcome to try."

Lacy sat down at the magic mirror and gazed into it. She started smiling and tears came to her eyes.

"Owen," she whispered. "I love you."

"Lacy, how is this possible?" asked Owen. He had been combing his hair in the bathroom in the barracks.

"I am looking in the magic mirror in Denton. I read about it in the paper and I was hoping I would see you one more time before you shipped out," said Lacy.

"You look wonderful," said Owen.

"How can I look wonderful with tears all over my face?" asked Lacy.

"To me you will always look wonderful. I love you. You take care of yourself. Write to me. I'll answer when I can. I'll see you when I get back." The mirror faded back to glass.

Lacy raised her tear-stained face to look at Will and her friend Marion.

"It worked," she said. "I saw Owen." Marion came over and hugged her.

Will smiled at her. "I take it Owen is in the service," he said.

"Yes, he is being shipped out tomorrow. If I hadn't seen him tonight, I wouldn't have seen him for two years. Thank you so much."

"Don't thank me. Thank the magic mirror," said Will.

Lacy turned and looked in the magic mirror again. "Thank you so much for letting me see Owen," said Lacy.

There was a soft flash of light inside the mirror.

Lacy gasped and then she smiled. "It said you are welcome," said Lacy with a smile.

She and Marion told Will and Tim goodbye and left to head home.

Tim looked at Will and smiled. Valerie came over and joined them.

"Thank you both for coming in. It was getting to be more than I could handle. You handle them very well, Will."

Will flushed slightly at this praise. "I love working here at the museum. You can call on me any time you need help," he said.

"I'll keep it in mind," said Valerie as she told both Will and Tim goodnight and went to see about closing the museum for the day.

Will and Tim left to return to the dorm and their homework. They were very happy that Lacy had seen her true love in the magic mirror.

Everything was ready for the wedding. Barring last minute details, everyone was satisfied with all they had accomplished. David had taken Amos and fitted him out with a child-sized tux. They wanted him to be a part of the ceremony. He was very proud, strutting around in his tux.

Lucy had agreed to keep Amos while they were gone. She was going to take him to daycare each day and pick him up after work. Charlie had assured them he would be visiting Amos while they were gone. Amos had told Lucy, Cam and Charlie about his car bed. He was very happy to have a big boy bed.

Charlie agreed to escort both Bertha and Janice down the aisle. Will was serving as Mike's best man and Cam was serving as David's. Brianna was Janice's maid-of-honor. Bertha asked her friend, Marge, from the police station to serve as her maid-of-honor.

The tents had been set up and chairs had been arranged. Doug's sister had arranged ribbons and bows along the inside edge of the rows of chairs. They had set up a stage and arranged flowers around. It looked like they were getting married in a flower garden.

The ladies from church had begun bringing food over and storing it in the house. It was to be taken out on the day of the wedding.

Lucy had arranged for a baker in town to make them a large wedding cake. It had a bride and groom on each side and a small boy in the middle. All of them loved the idea of including Amos. It made everything perfect for all of them.

Both couples had sessions with the pastor, and he was ready to perform the ceremonies.

Mike had asked Janice where she wanted to go on their honeymoon. She thought about it for a bit before answering: "I would like to stroll down Broadway and see a couple of shows. I want to walk in Central Park and eat hot dogs from a street vendor. The rest of the time, I want to snuggle up to my new husband and make love forever." She stopped talking because her mouth was otherwise occupied.

When they came up for air, Mike took his phone and made reservations in New York, bought some tickets for a couple of shows. He bought round trip airline tickets and arranged for flowers to be in their suite when they arrived.

Janice listened in awe. When he hung up his phone, she shook her head. "I tell you my wishes and five minutes later it is all arranged. If I weren't already in love with you, I would fall in love now."

Mike laughed. "I just want you to be happy. If you are happy, then I am happy. I love you. You are the light in my life. I am going to spend the rest of my life showing you how much I love you."

Janice snuggled closer and raised her face for his kiss.

CHAPTER 15

The wedding went smoothly. Everything happened when it was supposed to happen. Amos had been thrilled to be included in the ceremony. The cake had been cut. The part with the brides and grooms had been divided and saved for each couple. The little boy had been included in David and Bertha's share. David had signed the papers his lawyer had drawn up for Amos' adoption the day before. There would be a hearing when they returned from their honeymoon.

David and Mike had hired a limo and driver to take them all to the airport to catch their flights, one to Florida and one to New York. They did not want to leave their cars in the airport parking for a week. Cam and Charlie had both volunteered to drive them, but they wanted to spoil their new brides. They drank champagne and toasted to their new life. They separated at the airport and caught their different flights. All four of them were floating on clouds of happiness.

The day after the wedding, Brianna caught a flight to pack up her things and return to Denton. Since her records had been transferred and her financial aid had been approved, she was all ready to move to a new college and start a new life with her sister and her sister's new husband. She was thrilled to be included in this large and loving family. Most of all, she was going to be close to Tim. They could get to know more about each other. The lovely sizzle she got when she was around him didn't hurt. She thought with a smile.

Since he had a few days off, Will went by the museum to check on the new display. He and Tim had made up two more displays since they had designed the first one. Valerie was not in the front when he entered. One of the helpers was there.

"Hi, is Mrs. Drake around?" he asked.

"Yes, she went into her office to make a phone call," said the helper.

Will wandered around looking to see how people were taking the new displays. He heard some good comments and some not so good. He went on into the room with the magic mirror. There was a crowd of girls there, but at least they were being polite and taking turns with the mirror.

When he entered, a girl was talking to someone in the mirror, someone only she could see.

Will smiled. "Have many girls seen someone in the mirror?" he asked one of the girls in line.

"About half of them have seen someone," said the girl with a smile. "Even if I don't see someone today, I'll be back again. It is fun to try, and it gives us hope for a future with love."

"Yes," agreed Will. "Good luck." He turned and wandered on around to see if he could spot Valerie.

Valerie came out of her office and spotted Will. She smiled and made her way over to him.

The new displays are working out nicely," she said. "I haven't had this much interest in the museum since I took over."

Will smiled. "The magic mirror is doing better. I guess it didn't like all of the fussing around it."

Valerie laughed. "The mirror has very strong opinions. It has changed since you started dealing with it." Valerie looked at Will. She studied him seriously for a minute.

"What is it?" asked Will.

"Your time here is almost up. I was wondering how you liked working here," said Valerie.

"I love working here. It's the kind of job I was hoping to be able to find. I have always been interested in art and creativity," said Will.

"How would you like to keep working here as my assistant?" asked Valerie.

"I would love to," responded Will with a big smile.

"I talked to Mr. Ames. He is the owner of the museum. It is okay with him. I want to train you to take over when I take my maternity leave. I thought maybe you could switch most of your classes to online classes. The ones you have to go in to take, we can work around," Valerie paused and studied Will to see how he was taking her suggestion.

Will was stunned. He had no idea Valerie was even pregnant. To be offered his dream job was a lot to take in at once.

"What do you think?" asked Valerie.

"I think you are my fairy godmother. I never thought I would be able to get my dream job without having to leave home," said Will.

Valerie laughed. She was satisfied with Will's reaction.

"We'll work out the details later," said Valerie. "Maybe you should go and talk to your parents and be sure they have no objection."

"I'll do that after I talk to the magic mirror and let it know what is going on," said Will.

"Okay," agreed Valerie with a smile. She motioned for Will to go to the room with the magic mirror.

When Will entered the room with the magic mirror, most of the girls had looked into the mirror and left the museum. There were only two left. Will waited patiently while the last two girls looked in the mirror and left. After they were gone, he sat down in front of the magic mirror.

"Hello," said Will. "You and I have been through a lot together. Some of it I enjoyed, some of it was extremely painful. I'm not complaining. I know I deserved your retaliation. I wanted to talk to you today because Mrs. Drake has offered me a job here in the museum. It is a dream come true for me. Art and being around it has always been my true love. I think I have plenty of time to meet a girl. Now I have a chance to build a life for when the girl comes my way. I guess what I am trying to say is I'm going to be around. You and I are going to explore life together. When my true love does show up, I will leave it up to you to bring us together. For now, it is just you and me, pal." Will stopped and stared into the magic mirror. It flashed a light at him. Will smiled as he rose to leave.

He was ready to face his parents. What could they say? After all, the magic mirror had given its approval.

The End

ABOUT THE AUTHOR

With five children, ten grandchildren and six great-grandchildren I have a very busy life but reading and writing have always been a very large and enjoyable part of my life. I have been writing since I was very young. I kept notebooks, with my stories in them, private. I didn't share them with anyone. They were all hand-written because I was unable to type. We lived in the country and I had to do most of my writing at night. My days were busy helping with my brothers and sister. I also helped Mom with the garden and canning food for our family. Even though I was tired, I still managed to get my thoughts down on paper at night.

When I married and began raising my family, I continued writing my stories while helping my children through school and into their own lives and families. My sister was the only one to read my stories. She was very encouraging. When my youngest daughter started college, I decided to go to college myself. I had taken my GED at an earlier date and only had to take a class to pass my college entrance tests. I passed with flying colors and even managed to get a partial scholarship. I took computer classes to learn typing. The English Language and Literature classes helped me to polish my stories.

I found public speaking was not for me. I was much more comfortable with the written word but researching and writing the speeches was helpful. I could use information to build a story. I still managed to put my own spin on the essays.

I finished college with an associate degree and a 3.4 GPA. I had several awards including President's list, Dean's list, and Faculty list. The school experience helped me gain more confidence in my writing. I want to thank my English teacher in college for giving me more confidence in my writing by telling me that I had a good imagination. She said I told an interesting story. My daughter, who is a very good writer and has books of her own published, convinced me to have some of my stories published. She had them published for me. The first time I held one of my books in my hands and looked at my name on it as author, I was so proud. They were very well received. This was encouragement enough to convince me to continue writing and publishing. I have been building my library of books written by Betty McLain since then. I also wrote and illustrated several children's books.

Being able to type my stories opened up a whole new world for me. Having access to a computer helped me to look up anything I needed to know and expanded my ability to keep writing my books. Joining Facebook and making friends all over the world expanded my outlook considerably. I was able to understand many different lifestyles and incorporate them in my ideas.

I have heard the saying, watch out what you say and don't make the writer mad, you may end up in a book being eliminated. It is true. All of life is there to stimulate your imagination. It is fun to sit and think about how a thought can be changed to develop a story, and to watch the story develop and come alive in your mind. When I get started, the stories almost write themselves, I just have to get all of it down as I think it before it is gone.

I love knowing the stories I have written are being read and enjoyed by others. It is awe inspiring to look at the books and think I wrote that.

I look forward to many more years of putting my stories out there and hope the people reading my books are looking forward to reading them as much.

Lightning Source UK Ltd.
Milton Keynes UK
UKHW010640160920
370007UK00001B/134